Praise for
JAMES PATTERSON

Praise for BECOMING MUHAMMAD ALI

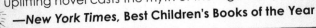

"Cassius Clay's kinetic boyhood—depicted through prose, poetry, and illustration—is the prism through which this uplifting novel casts the myth of the legendary boxer."
—**New York Times, Best Children's Books of the Year**

"This utterly delightful story about Ali's childhood is a smash hit. Get this uplifting, informative book onto library shelves and into kids' hands."
—**School Library Journal, starred review**

"Patterson and Alexander, two heavyweights in the world of books, unite to tell the story of how Cassius Clay grew up to be Muhammad Ali, one of the greatest boxers of all time."
—**The Horn Book, starred review**

"The prose and poems reflect Clay's public bravado and private humbleness as well as his appreciation and respect for family and friends. A knockout!"
—**Booklist, starred review**

"Spare...witty...Cassius's narrative illustrates his charisma [and] drive...Powerful, accessible view of a fascinating figure."
—**Publishers Weekly, starred review**

"A stellar collaboration that introduces an important and intriguing individual to today's readers."
—**Kirkus Reviews, starred review**

"These lightning-bolt figures are poetry surrounded by prose...a kinetic, dazzling experience...Like the world many adolescents inhabit, the world that Becoming Muhammad Ali presents is complex...But most importantly, it's a reminder that once upon a time Cassius Clay, all poetry and italics, was a kid like the rest of us. It is my hope that Black children read this book, see themselves in young Clay and know that they too are poetry made flesh."
—**New York Times Book Review**

Praise for the **MAXIMUM RIDE** Series

School's Out—Forever

"Readers are in for another exciting, wild ride."
—Kirkus Reviews

Praise for the **MIDDLE SCHOOL** Series

Middle School, The Worst Years of My Life

"A keen appreciation of kids' insecurities and an even more astute understanding of what might propel boy readers through a book...a perfectly pitched novel."
—Los Angeles Times

"Cleverly delves into the events that make middle school so awkward: cranky bus drivers, tardy slips, bathroom passes, and lots of rules."
—Associated Press

Praise for the **JACKY HA-HA** Series

Jacky Ha-Ha

"A strong female protagonist, realistic characters, and a balanced approach to middle-school life make this book a winner."
—Common Sense Media

"James Patterson has figured out the formula for writing entertaining books for tween readers."
—Parents' Choice

JIMMY PATTERSON BOOKS
FOR YOUNG READERS

James Patterson Presents

Sci-Fi Junior High by John Martin and Scott Seegert

Sci-Fi Junior High: Crash Landing by John Martin and Scott Seegert

How to Be a Supervillain by Michael Fry

How to Be a Supervillain: Born to Be Good by Michael Fry

How to Be a Supervillain: Bad Guys Finish First by Michael Fry

The Unflushables by Ron Bates

Ernestine, Catastrophe Queen by Merrill Wyatt

Scouts by Shannon Greenland

No More Monsters Under Your Bed! by Jordan Chouteau

There Was an Old Woman Who Lived in a Book by Jomike Tejido

The Ugly Doodles by Valeria Wicker

Sweet Child O' Mine by Guns N' Roses

The Family that Cooks Together by Anna and Madeline Zakarian, daughters of Geoffrey Zakarian

The Day the Kids Took Over by Sam Apple

If Kids Could Drive by Marisa Kollmeier and Teepoo Riaz

The Middle School Series by James Patterson

Middle School, The Worst Years of My Life

Middle School: Get Me Out of Here!

Middle School: Big Fat Liar

Middle School: How I Survived Bullies, Broccoli, and Snake Hill

Middle School: Ultimate Showdown

Middle School: Save Rafe!

Middle School: Just My Rotten Luck

Middle School: Dog's Best Friend

Middle School: Escape to Australia

Middle School: From Hero to Zero

Middle School: Born to Rock

Middle School: Master of Disaster

Middle School: Field Trip Fiasco

For exclusives, trailers, and other information,
visit jimmypatterson.org.

JAMES PATTERSON BOOKS FOR YOUNG READERS AWARDS AND NOMINATIONS

THE MIDDLE SCHOOL SERIES

A Young Adult Library Services Association Quick Pick for Reluctant Young Adult Readers
A Children's Choice Book Award Nominee for Author of the Year
A #1 *New York Times* Bestseller
A #1 Indiebound Bestseller
A Nēnē Hawaii Children's Choice Award Winner
An Association for Library Service to Children Summer Reading List Book
A Delaware Diamonds Book Award Winner
An Oregon Children's Choice Award Winner
An Oregon Reader's Choice Award Nominee
A Wisconsin Golden Archer Award Nominee
A Pacific Northwest Young Reader's Choice Award Nominee
A Wyoming Soaring Eagle Book Award Nominee

THE I FUNNY SERIES

A #1 *New York Times* Bestseller
A Maryland Black-Eyed Susan Book Award Winner
A Dorothy Canfield Fisher Award Nominee
A Colorado Children's Choice Award Nominee

THE JACKY HA-HA SERIES

A #1 *New York Times* Bestseller
A Parents' Choice Award Winner
A National Parenting Products Award Winner

THE TREASURE HUNTERS SERIES

A #1 *New York Times* Bestseller

THE HOUSE OF ROBOTS SERIES

A #1 *New York Times* Bestseller

THE DANIEL X SERIES

A #1 *New York Times* Bestseller
A Louisiana Young Readers Choice Award Nominee
A Florida Sunshine State Young Readers' Award Nominee

WORD OF MOUSE

A Young Hoosier Award Nominee
A New York State Reading Association Charlotte Award Nominee
A Louisiana Young Readers' Choice Award Nominee

WORLD CHAMPIONS!

A MAX EINSTEIN ADVENTURE

JAMES PATTERSON
AND CHRiS GRABENSTEiN

Illustrated by Jay Fabares

JIMMY PATTERSON BOOKS
LITTLE, BROWN AND COMPANY
New York Boston London

Text copyright © 2021 by Zero Point Venture LLC.
Illustrations copyright © 2021 by Hachette Book Group, Inc.

JIMMY Patterson Books / Little, Brown and Company
Hachette Book Group
1290 Avenue of the Americas, New York, NY 10104
JamesPatterson.com
First Edition: August 2021

JIMMY Patterson Books is an imprint of Little, Brown and Company, a division of Hachette Book Group, Inc. The Little, Brown name and logo are trademarks of Hachette Book Group, Inc. The JIMMY Patterson Books® name and logo are trademarks of JBP Business, LLC.

The Hachette Speakers Bureau provides a wide range of authors for speaking events. To find out more, go to hachettespeakersbureau.com or call (866) 376-6591.

Library of Congress Cataloging-in-Publication Data has been applied for.

ISBN: 978-0-759-55692-8 (hc)

Printing 1, 2021

Printed in the United States of America

WORLD
CHAMPIONS!
A MAX EINSTEIN ADVENTURE

The Story So Far...

MAX EINSTEIN is not your typical twelve-year-old genius.

She hacked the computer system at NYU so she could attend college classes. She built inventions to help the homeless people she lived with.

She talks with her hero Albert Einstein. (Okay, that's just in her imagination.)

But everything changed when Max, a homeless orphan who could barely remember meeting her parents, was recruited by a mysterious organization known as the Change Makers Institute. Their mission: solve some of the world's

toughest problems using science and smarts. She led a diverse group of young geniuses from around the globe as they worked to solve humanity's biggest problems.

But they can only continue to do good in the world if they can continue to outfox the forces of greed.

And those forces aren't going away anytime soon.

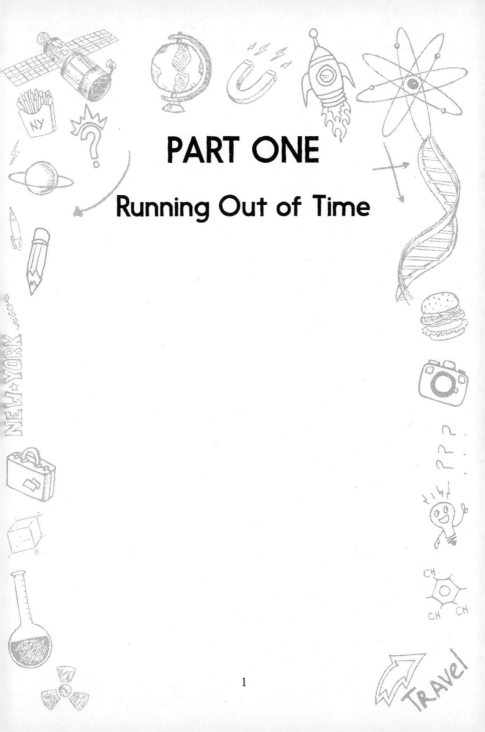

PART ONE

Running Out of Time

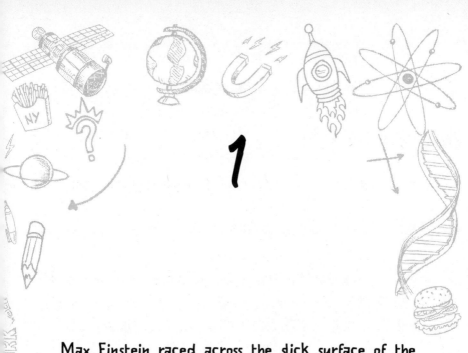

1

Max Einstein raced across the slick surface of the glacier wishing she had worn something warmer than her flapping trench coat.

Wishing she could somehow run faster, that her bulging backpack wasn't slowing her down.

Wishing some angry crew of mysterious mercenaries wasn't chasing after her and Siobhan.

The ice rapidly melting beneath Max's feet created snaking rivulets of turquoise blue water that widened into streams that sliced through the ice and made gaping holes that ended up as gushing waterfalls.

The frozen tundra was melting.

"We don't have much time, Max!" shouted her friend and colleague, the twelve-year-old geoscientist (and certified genius) Siobhan.

Max realized that the fiery redhead could be talking about the earth *or* their current predicament. Both were true.

They had been examining the Jakobshavn Glacier on the west coast of Greenland because global warming was causing its ice to disappear at an alarming rate. It was turning the once-solid Greenland Ice Sheet into a melting slab of leaky Swiss cheese. Benjamin Franklin Abercrombie, the billionaire backer of the CMI, had sent Max and Siobhan to this glacier in Greenland to research the team's next big assignment: turning around the world's climate crisis.

Max and Siobhan were also running out of time because a mysterious team of thugs in white camouflage (which made them look like Darth Vader's stormtroopers) was pursuing the two friends on sleek, glistening white gas-powered snowmobiles with skids that could churn across the slippery surface much better than the soles of Max's and Siobhan's hiking boots.

They also had rifles.

"We should lose these bloomin' backpacks!" Siobhan shouted, tugging at the straps. "They're slowin' us down."

"No!" Max shouted back. "But let me rip out the zipper."

"*What?*"

Max dug into the deep pockets of her trench coat to grab her Swiss Army knife. She flicked it open and, with a few swift slices, cut out the strip of bumpy zipper teeth. She separated the two sides and handed the pair of nubby fabric strands to Siobhan. "Tie these around your feet. They'll give you better traction. Like cleats or snow chains for tires."

Siobhan quickly lashed the grip strips around her boots while Max ripped out the zipper in her backpack and improvised her own pair of slip-proof running shoes.

"Friction is our friend!" said Max. "Let's go."

They took off. The running was a little easier; a little less slip-n-slide.

But the goons with guns had those snowmobiles. They were gaining on Max and Siobhan, quickly closing the gap in the race across the icy plateau.

Now Max wished Ben hadn't "terminated" the CMI's security detail, Charl and Isabl. He thought the team didn't need armed guards anymore since the evil Corp was currently out of business.

"Who are these bloomin' idjits chasing after us?" Siobhan

seethed. "I thought the Corp was over and done for. Who wants to stop us now?"

Lots of people, thought Max. *You make dealing with global warming your top priority, you're gonna make a whole lot of very wealthy, very powerful people very angry.*

Suddenly, Max heard something louder than the roar of the rushing water boring through the melting ice. The *whomp-whomp-whomp* of chopper blades as a sleek black helicopter rose up on the bright blue horizon, clearing the edge of the glacier just as another huge slab of ice and snow let loose and crashed into the sea.

And yeah, the guys inside the helicopter were decked out in the same snow camo as the guys on the snowmobiles. They also had the same kind of weapons.

"We've definitely run out of time!" cried Siobhan.

"We've also run out of glacier!" Max shouted back.

They were racing straight toward an icy cliff. There was nothing ahead of them but blue sky and thin, wispy clouds.

"We need to jump!" said Max.

"Off a bloomin' glacier? Bad idea!"

Max agreed. "Terrible idea! But it's the only one we have left."

Max and Siobhan reached the end of the ice.

"Jump!" said Max.

"I thought we were supposed to be smart," said Siobhan.

"Geniuses," added Max.

And then the two friends closed their eyes and jumped off the icy bluff.

2

Three seconds later, Max gave Siobhan another command.

"Now!"

Max yanked hard on the rip cord attached to her backpack. Siobhan did the same.

A pair of small, tactical parachutes exploded out of their backpacks and caught the arctic air. Max and Siobhan, of course, both totally understood the physics of their low-altitude jump: air resistance buffeting the chute would overwhelm the downward force of gravity, transferring their net force and acceleration upward. The two skydivers slowed down. As their speed decreased, the air resistance

also decreased until Max and Siobhan were just floating over the chilly blue waters of Greenland's Baffin Bay.

"We've reached terminal velocity," Max announced.

"Thank goodness those two haven't!" said Siobhan in her lilting Irish accent. She gestured down to a rapidly approaching boat skimming across the surface of the water, gunning for the spot where Max and Siobhan were about to splash down.

On board was another member of the CMI team—Klaus, the sausage-loving robotics expert from Poland. But he wasn't the one piloting the boat. That job was being deftly handled by Leo, the CMI's amazing automaton. Klaus was just along for the ride and to make sure the robot's circuits stayed dry.

Triangulating and timing his approach perfectly, Leo positioned the mini ice-cutting craft right where Max and Siobhan needed it for a pinpoint, deck-rocking landing.

"Thanks, you guys," said Max, peeling off her backpack when she and Siobhan were safely on board.

"Appreciate the on-time arrival," added Siobhan as she undid her parachute.

"We were tracking you across the ice," said Klaus. "You guys were moving fast."

"May I inquire as to why you needed to execute such a dramatic extraction from the iceberg?" said Leo in his clipped, robotic voice. "After all, Ben charged you two with gathering geographical data for our upcoming—"

Max held up her hand to silence Leo and pointed behind him. "That's why."

The pack of snowmobiles had reached the craggy bluff of the glacier.

"We were runnin' away from those blokes," said Siobhan.

"And those," said Max as the helicopter hovered up and over the glacier again. "We don't know who they are—just that they don't want us snooping around on melting glaciers."

"Leo?" said Klaus, squinting up as the chopper cleared the crest of the frigid cliff and dropped down to chase after the CMI's tiny ice-cutting craft. "Execute *Ostatni Rów Awaryjny Manewr.*"

Max and Siobhan both had *huh?* expressions on their faces.

"It's Polish for 'Last Ditch Emergency Maneuver,'" said Klaus. "Grab hold of something and hang on."

Max and Siobhan braced themselves.

Leo jammed the throttle forward as the helicopter

hovered closer. A rifle shot reverberated off the walls of the towering glacier. The bullet zinged past the fleeing boat and sliced through the water.

"Initiating thermal scan," reported Leo.

"Are you doing what I think you're doing?" Max shouted to Klaus. She had to shout to be heard over the roar of the little boat's engine, the thrumming of the helicopter charging up behind them, and the strange straining groans from the walls of the blue-streaked glacier.

The glacier Leo was heading straight for.

Klaus nodded.

More shots rang out. One bullet dinged the metal bow of the boat.

"Klaus, you lunkhead, override the bot!" shrieked Siobhan. "We're going to slam right into that wall of ice!"

"No, we're not," insisted Klaus. "Right, Leo?"

"Correct," Leo (who looked like a grinning department store mannequin in the boys' wear section) calmly replied. "Right full rudder!"

He gave the wheel a wicked twist to the right.

The small boat lurched to the side and skirted along the glacier. They were so close, Max felt as if she'd just stuck her head into a frosted-over freezer.

The helicopter followed in hot pursuit. It banked into a right turn and chased after the boat, the tips of its whirling blades flicking against the screeching glacier wall, sending up a chilly spray of ice chips.

"Wait for it..." said Leo.

The glacier seemed to groan even louder.

"It's calving," said Leo, using the technical term for a glacier shedding sheets of blocky ice. "Right full rudder!" He swung the boat into another hard turn, streaking away from the glacier just as it let go and tumbled down in a massive avalanche of ice.

The helicopter probably wanted to make the same hard right turn. But it was too late.

The crumbling wall of ice crashed into its rotors and shattered the glass bubble of the cockpit.

Whoever had been chasing after Max Einstein and her Change Maker Institute friends was now sinking down into the rising sea—right alongside a massive chunk of Greenland's endangered ice sheet.

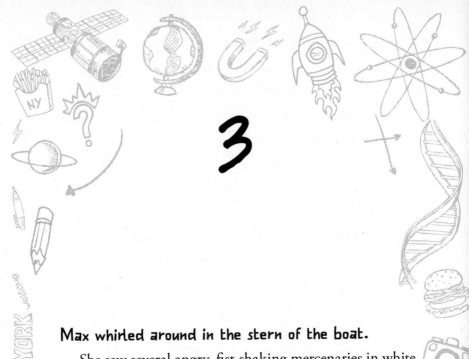

3

Max whirled around in the stern of the boat.

She saw several angry, fist-shaking mercenaries in white camo bobbing up and down in the icy water where the chopper went down.

"They're okay," she said, relieved. "And they probably have their own recovery team..."

"Maybe," said Klaus. "But I bet they're not as good as me and Leo!"

Leo throttled the small boat's engine and raced away from the glacier.

The automaton had become such a trustworthy member of the CMI team, it was sometimes hard for Max to

remember that the boy-bot with the molded plastic face had originally worked for (and was created by) the Corp to help them hunt down Max Einstein.

Back then he was called Lenard—probably because Dr. Zimm, who used to be Max's number one nemesis, knew that Philipp Lenard had been one of Albert Einstein's big-time antagonists. Dr. Zimm also knew that Max idolized Professor Einstein. Always had. Always would.

But, during their last major project, Max and her team had exposed Dr. Zimm and the other very powerful members of a shadowy, secret organization called the Corp to the public. The group had been disbanded and totally shut down. Their West Virginia headquarters, located inside a creepy cave, was gone—all its files and data carted off by various investigators from countries all around the globe. Dr. Zimm was no longer a threat. The Corp no longer existed.

But somebody had just chased Max and Siobhan across the slick surface of a melting glacier.

Who?

Why?

"Thanks for being there to save our bacon," Siobhan said to Leo.

"Bacon?" said Leo. "I don't recall encountering break-fast meat during our rendezvous and rescue mission."

Leo's hard-core logic made Max and Siobhan laugh. Laughing felt good. Much better than running for your life.

"I coded all that heroic action-movie stuff into Leo's hard drive," boasted Klaus. "But what happened back at that glacier is bad news, Max. The Corp is kaput but, all of a sudden, you have new enemies?" He shook his head. "Bad, man. Bad."

"Whoever they were," said Siobhan, "they were undoubt-edly bought and paid for by some money-grubbing pack of climate change deniers." She looked like she had a bad taste in her mouth.

"Whoa," said Klaus. "Who says climate change is responsible for what's happening to those glaciers? It's sum-mer. Sure there's a bunch of surface meltwater and ice shed-ding because, hello? *It's summer.* Here's a little Einsteinian thought experiment for you, Max. Put an ice cube in a beam of sunshine. What do you think's gonna happen? It's gonna melt!"

Max gave Klaus an honestly quizzical look. "You really believe this is all a hoax?"

"Uh, yeah."

"Then, congratulations. You're my new challenge."

"We already have enough of a challenge," said Siobhan. "The planet is running out of time and we need to fix it—whether Klaus is with us or not."

"Not," said Klaus, crossing his arms defiantly over his chest.

"I hope you'll change your mind," said Max. "Because there is no Planet B."

"Oh, now you're quoting T-shirts at me?" snorted Klaus. "Ha! Brilliant, Max. Brilliant."

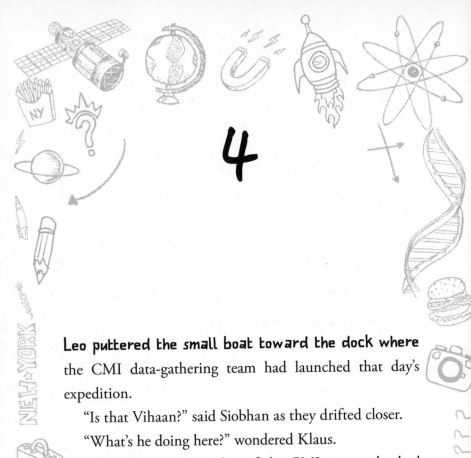

4

Leo puttered the small boat toward the dock where the CMI data-gathering team had launched that day's expedition.

"Is that Vihaan?" said Siobhan as they drifted closer.

"What's he doing here?" wondered Klaus.

Vihaan, another member of the CMI team, who had been busy managing the group's water purification efforts back home in India, waved both arms over his head. He was dressed in a kurta, a loose collarless shirt. Vihaan Banerjee was only thirteen, but he'd already earned a university degree in quantum mechanics. He also hoped to, one day,

develop a U.T.O.E.—a unified theory of everything—that would explain all physical aspects of the universe.

Something that Max knew Albert Einstein had always wanted to do.

Klaus tossed Vihaan a rope line.

"What are you doing here?" Klaus asked.

"It's urgent," Vihaan replied. "Ben is assembling the entire team in Miami. He sent a jet to pick me up in Mumbai. I am to bring you four with me to Florida."

"Great," said Siobhan, as the boat crew climbed onto the dock. "Here we are tryin' to deal with global warming, but we're fixin' to blaze through the sky in a private jet that, of course, spews out carbon dioxide and other disgusting greenhouse gases?"

"Not this jet," said Vihaan. "It's brand-new and powered by quantum solar cells. Zero carbon emissions."

"Solar powered?" said Klaus, sounding horrified. "What if it flies through a cloud? Do the engines just quit?"

"Um, no," Vihaan said with a slight chuckle. "It has these things called batteries?"

While Klaus and Vihaan went back and forth about the solar-powered jet, Max thought about Albert Einstein's

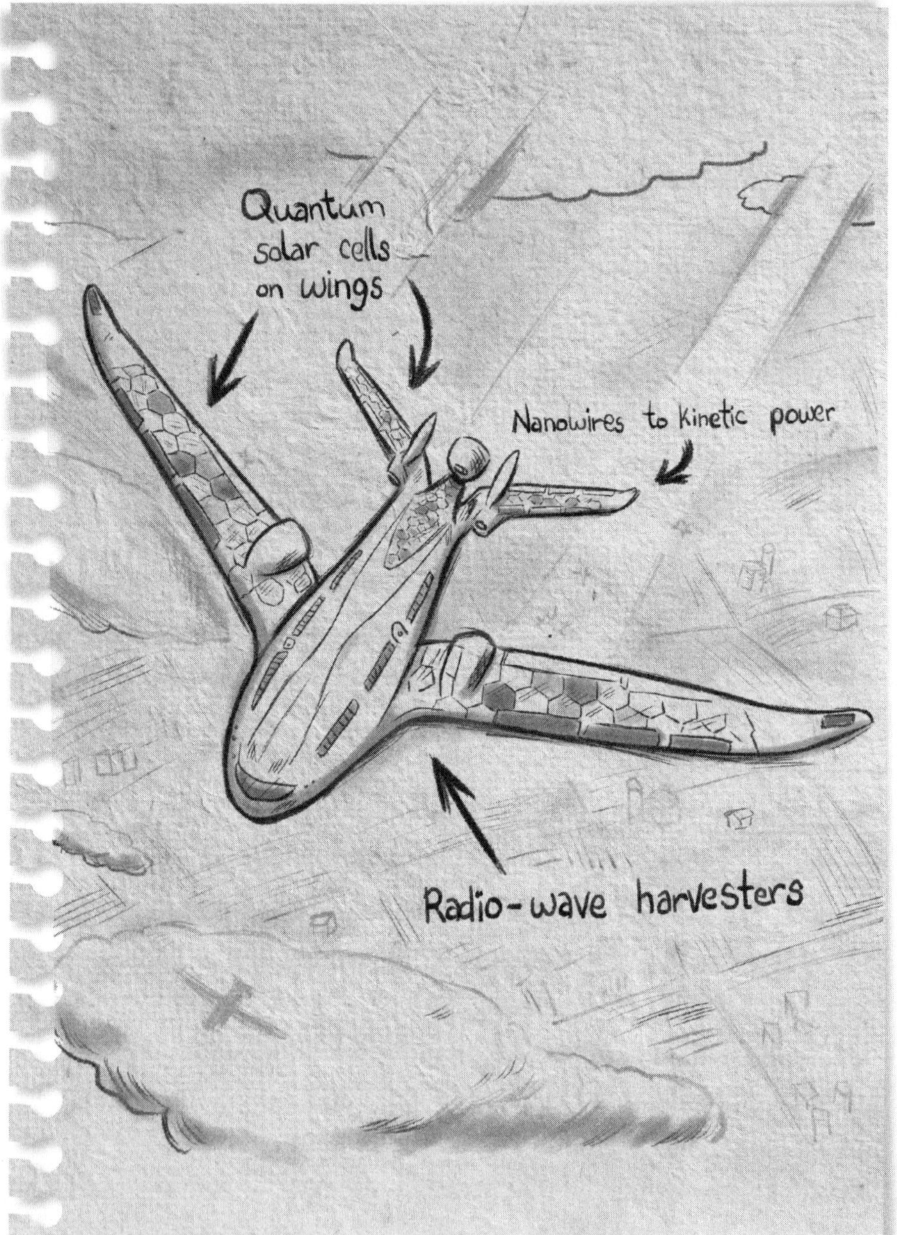
Quantum solar cells on wings
Nanowires to kinetic power
Radio-wave harvesters

1921 Nobel Prize, which he won, in part, for his "discovery of the law of the photoelectric effect."

Yep. Back in 1921, the emission of electrons from an illuminated surface had been a theory. But, eventually, that theory led to electricity being generated by solar panels. And now, a solar-powered jet aircraft.

Max realized that big leaps were often just the end result of a series of small steps. She just hoped that she and her teammates could take all the right steps to help save the planet—before it was too late.

Because the earth's doomsday clock was definitely ticking.

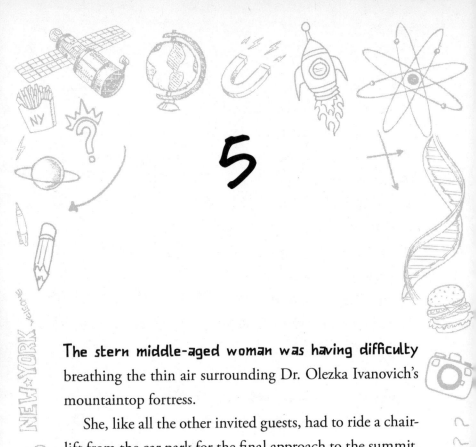

5

The stern middle-aged woman was having difficulty breathing the thin air surrounding Dr. Olezka Ivanovich's mountaintop fortress.

She, like all the other invited guests, had to ride a chairlift from the car park for the final approach to the summit. Although she'd visited Russia before, she much preferred Moscow to the desolate isolation of these Ural Mountains near Bashkortostan.

But, she realized, Dr. Ivanovich was such a genius he knew exactly where to place his secret fortress. If the oceans were truly going to rise (as all the gloom-and-doom global warming alarmists insisted), then the Urals were the perfect place to build. In time, the slopes of this craggy, 1,600-meter mountain might even become beautiful beachfront property.

A group of soldiers decked out in white camouflage uniforms checked the woman's identification papers at the top of the chairlift. She then lined up behind all the others waiting to pass through the metal detector before entering Dr. Ivanovich's top-secret compound. She recognized several of the dignitaries ahead of her. They were all major players from the fossil fuel industry and the world of high finance. Powerful funders of the global anti-climate-change coalition.

All of them were betting on Dr. Ivanovich—a man with a mind to rival that of Albert Einstein himself—and his secretive Okamenelosti Group to lead them into a future that was a carbon copy of its past. None of these gray-haired titans of industry and commerce wanted anything to change. They had so much more money to make sucking the earth's resources dry.

Once she'd been scanned and cleared, the woman made her way into the renovated fortress where she was greeted by one of several gruff men and women in blue blazers, all with listening devices jammed into their ears, interviewing each arrival. Most of the guests were champions of fossil fuel. Worldwide leaders of the climate change denial movement. All of them very rich, very powerful people.

"You are Ms. Tari Kaplan?" her assigned man asked, consulting his sleek tablet computer.

"That is correct," the woman replied, stiffening slightly.

"You were the Corp's mole inside the so-called Change Makers Institute?"

"Correct again. I started in the CMI's Jerusalem headquarters and moved on to field operations."

"Alas," said the man, perhaps sarcastically, "the Corp is no more."

Ms. Kaplan managed a smile. "Alas."

"We welcome you to the Okamenelosti. Dr. Ivanovich may wish to ask you a few questions following the presentation. In private. A return on his, shall we say, investment in you?"

"Of course," said Ms. Kaplan. "It would be my honor."

The man clicked his heels and made a swooping gesture toward the grand lobby where the audience was already starting to shuffle into the mountain retreat's mammoth auditorium, many of them bringing their flutes of champagne and small plates of caviar with them.

"*Spasibo*," Ms. Kaplan told her security guard interrogator, using the Russian word for "thank you."

She also knew that other Russian word. The name of Dr. Ivanovich's group. The Okamenelosti.

It meant "the fossils." Not because so many members of the wealthy group had wrinkled skin and gray hair. Because so many of them made so much money off coal, oil, and natural gas—the concentrated organic compounds in the earth's crust that had made modern life possible.

Ms. Kaplan skipped the elegant refreshment tables and entered the posh auditorium. She found an empty seat on the aisle, down near the stage. The other 299 red velvet chairs around her were filled quickly.

Finally, the lights dimmed and Dr. Olezka Ivanovich, the genius himself, strode, somewhat awkwardly, onto the stage where he was illuminated by a dusty spotlight. The famed intellectual giant had wild black hair, a bristle brush mustache, and slumped shoulders. His eyes were narrow and dark. One hand was stuffed into the baggy coat pocket of his three-piece tweed suit. The other hand was fidgeting with a pair of clacking balls about the size of robin eggs. When the spotlight glinted off their faceted faces,

Ms. Kaplan realized that the objects Dr. Ivanovich was rolling around between his fingers weren't classic "worry balls" made of steel. They were two egg-sized diamonds.

"Welcome, my friends," Dr. Ivanovich said to the crowd. He had a slight Russian accent. "I see that the ranks of the Okamenelosti have swollen somewhat since our last annual conference." He smiled at some oil men in the front row wearing cowboy boots. "I am so sorry that so many of you wasted so much of your time and money hoping that the Corp, may they rest in peace, would, somehow, deliver a more glorious future. Unfortunately, they did not. In fact, they are no more. Wiped off the face of the earth by a crusading band of activist children. How sad. But do not despair, ladies and gentlemen. You are now in precisely the right place."

The audience applauded enthusiastically.

"As we all know, the earth still has at least fifty years of crude oil reserves remaining beneath its crust. Natural gas will last us another ninety-two years, thanks to frack-ing. And, of course, we have one hundred and fifty years until our mountains run out of coal. It would be rude for us not to take all that Mother Earth has to offer. And why should countries, such as India, be deprived of a coal-fueled industrial revolution, much like the ones already enjoyed by England and America centuries ago?"

More applause.

Dr. Ivanovich rolled his diamonds around in his hand, positioning one between his thumb and forefinger. He held it up for the audience to admire. Light reflecting off the angled cuts on its face danced across the stage. "This flawless, one-hundred-and-eighteen-carat gem was once nothing but a lowly lump of rotting carbon buried deep within the earth. Look at it now! LOOK AT IT! I am told it is worth thirty-five million American dollars. Thirty-five million... and I have two."

The audience chuckled.

"From carbon comes great wealth, ladies and gentlemen. From carbon comes great power! From carbon comes great strength and beauty!"

The audience was on its feet.

"And nothing will stop us," Dr. Ivanovich continued. "Not the Paris Accord. Not all the fake and phony science. And especially not the infantile, foolish, sentimental children of this world!" Now he was whipping the crowd into a frenzy. "Who are these sniveling little brats to tell their elders what to do with what we have worked so hard to achieve? Who are they to march out of their schools demanding action on this hoax of climate change? My friends, the children of this world need to be taught a lesson."

He turned again to the oilmen in their cowboy boots.

"Your beloved Corp wasted much time and energy trying to recruit the young Max Einstein and her merry band of so-called geniuses. Well, my friends, I am much smarter than all of those children combined. And trust me, the Okamenelosti shall not waste time attempting to court or recruit Max Einstein. No, my friends. We shall eliminate her!"

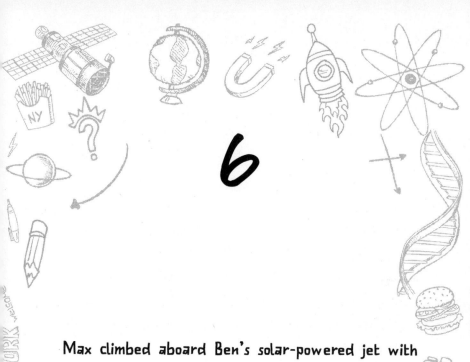

6

Max climbed aboard Ben's solar-powered jet with Klaus, Siobhan, and Vihaan.

Leo, the robot, would make the trip in the cargo compartment with the rest of the team's luggage and gear. It was the robot's idea.

"I need sleep time to crunch data," he'd said. "It's similar to your need for dreaming."

Max never traveled with much more than a small duffel bag and backpack. On the CMI's last mission, she'd lost her beloved (and battered) antique suitcase filled with all sorts of Einstein memorabilia.

The same suitcase she might've time-traveled inside from 1921.

Yeah. There was that one bit of her bio that she still didn't quite believe. While the CMI team was in Princeton, Max discovered that—maybe, possibly, she couldn't be one hundred percent sure—her parents, inspired by Albert Einstein's theory of relativity, had created (in their New Jersey basement, no less) a time machine that had accidentally sent the infant Max, and that suitcase, flying on fast-forward from 1921.

Having already climbed the fold-down airstairs, Max entered the futuristic jet's wide cabin.

"You must be Max," said an extremely cool-looking girl. She appeared to be a year or two older than Max, had a streak of purple hair, a nose ring, and big "smart girl" glasses.

"I'm Anna Sophia Fiorillo. You can call me Anna Sophia. Or Anna. I'm down with whatever. Most of my followers go with Anna. Faster to tap into their devices."

The perky girl thrust out her hand. Max shook it.

"Pleased to meet you."

Anna bounced up eagerly on the balls of her feet, which

were sporting a pair of very expensive sneakers. "Ben brought me on board," she said. "Guess you could say I'm the newest member of the CMI team."

Max wondered if Anna would be replacing Hana, the genius botanist who, more or less, betrayed Max and the whole CMI team while they were working in West Virginia. Hana had been in cahoots with Ms. Tari Kaplan, a stern middle-aged CMI staff person (who never really liked Max but loved to give tests). Max first met Ms. Kaplan at the CMI headquarters in Jerusalem.

For her traitorous acts, Hana had earned a one-way ticket home to Japan. In coach.

Ms. Kaplan, on the other hand, who totally sold Max and her team out to the Corp, was dealt with a little more severely. Max knew she'd been sent to jail, where she was probably awaiting trial. No way could she afford the bail money required to purchase her temporary freedom.

Because that bail was ten million dollars.

"What's your specialty?" Max asked the newcomer. "Botany like Hana?"

The girl laughed out of the corner of her mouth, making her purple-tipped hair flutter.

"Hardly. I'm not a science geek like you guys—no offense. Geeks are the new awesome. But I'm all about brand management and brand asset maximization. And Max Einstein? You're the asset we need to maximize. Go grab a seat, girlfriend. I'll bring you and the others up to speed once we reach a comfortable cruising altitude."

Max just nodded and found the nearest available seat. It was a plush swivel chair. Like something you'd find in a corporate boardroom, only it had a seat belt.

Max strapped herself in. Siobhan was in the seat across the aisle.

"So?" Siobhan whispered. "What do you think of Anna?"

"She seems nice enough…"

"She's super cool. I follow her on Instagram, Snapchat, and Twitter."

"Seriously?"

"Oh, yeah. Her YouTube channel is also pretty spectacular. Anna Sophia Fiorillo is a bloomin' phenom. A marketing genius. It's why she's one of the world's top ten teen influencers."

"Huh," said Max, realizing she should probably do more standard twelve-year-old stuff like social media instead of laser-focusing on science, Einstein, and saving the world. "Wonder what a marketing whiz is doing with us? How's she going to help us tackle global warming?"

Siobhan shrugged. "Guess we'll find out once we reach a comfortable cruising altitude."

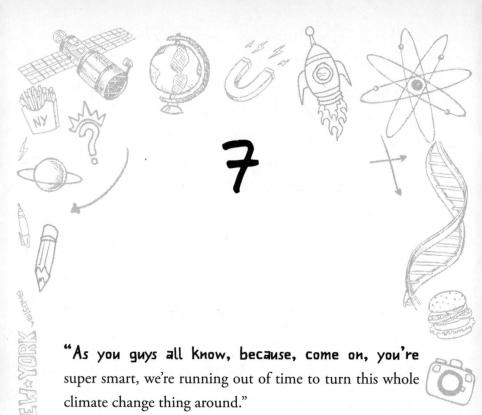

7

"As you guys all know, because, come on, you're super smart, we're running out of time to turn this whole climate change thing around."

Anna Sophia Fiorillo was standing at the front of the solar jet's cabin gesturing at a video screen filled with animated graphics and spinning images. Smokestacks belching out smoke. Smog in China. Polar bears stranded on floating chunks of ice. Out-of-control wildfires. Parched and crackled desert sand. Refugees on the move. The whole horror show of global warming.

"Now you brainiacs are in charge of coming up with the big solution, obviously. My job? To make sure the world

hears about it. That they know about it. That they feel it. You're already generating tremendous buzz, Max, after you shut down the bad guys in West Virginia."

"That was a team effort," said Max.

"It definitely was," said Klaus. "I know I sure played a major role on the robotics end of things."

"You all performed marvelously," added Vihaan. "As a result, the Corp quit interfering with my water purification efforts in India."

"We should've made more out of that thing in India," said Anna, shaking her head. "But, I know, I know. You guys were flying under the radar. Keeping everything you did super-secret."

"Because," said Siobhan, somewhat defensively, "as you might've heard, there was this little matter of the Corp trying to kidnap or kill Max."

"Maybe both," said Klaus, with an awkward laugh.

Anna rubbed her hands together. "Well, your days of hiding are over. Ben Abercrombie brought me on board to flip that switch. He thinks, and I totally agree, that we can get more good done by making more out of what good we get done. Max? You're our giant slayer."

"I'm just—"

"Whoa. Dial down the humility. You have a look that cuts through the cluttered media environment. You have a fantastic, semi-mysterious backstory. You took down this deeply evil shadow group the Corp? Boom! We go viral with video clips. We make memes. We give this movement a face."

Max sank down a little lower in her seat. Anna Fiorillo was looking directly at her.

"That's the plan, Max. You become the face of the CMI."

"Um, no thanks..."

"You've got the perfect look. That wild mop of red curls. That steely-eyed determination. That history of homelessness and going to college when you were just a kid..."

"Hey, I did that, too," said Klaus.

Fiorillo ignored him. "And that rumpled old trench coat you wear, Max? Mwah!" She kissed her fingers like she was a very pleased French chef. "You can't buy quirky, brandable individuality like that."

"Sure you can," cracked Siobhan. "Just go to any thrift shop selling frumpy old raincoats."

"Max, you need to be our Beyoncé," the marketing whiz continued. "The person out front, grabbing the spotlight. The rest of the CMI crew is like your band and background dancers."

Vihaan looked puzzled. Siobhan rolled her eyes. Klaus was getting that pouty jealous look on his pudgy face again.

"I am not a background dancer!" he protested. "I despise dancing. It's a complete waste of calories."

Max? No way did she want to become the public face of a global movement. She was an orphan. She never stayed in one place long enough for anybody to know who she was because she really didn't know that herself. She'd lived her childhood constantly on the move. She kept a low profile. Lived on the street. Avoided the authorities.

Now Ben and this hotshot social media influence expert wanted to make her famous? Turn her into the next Greta Thunberg with her face all over social media and magazine covers and YouTube?

No, thank you very much.

Too bad Anna Sophia Fiorillo couldn't've been a botanist.

8

Max had never flown on an aircraft as quiet as Ben's solar-powered jet.

Then again, she'd never flown on any aircraft until the Change Makers Institute recruited her to join their team. And now they wanted to make her the public face of the organization?

Fortunately, Anna Fiorillo's pitch and spiel had only lasted about an hour. When she flat-out asked Max if she'd be the spokesperson, Max had replied with a very noncommittal "I'll have to think about it."

"Sure, sure," Anna had replied. "Thinking is what you

guys do best. Making that thinking count? That's where I come in."

They were still two hours out from Miami.

Max propped a small pillow against a window and, leaning into it, tried to fall asleep. *If I have to look good on TV, I need my beauty rest.* The thought made her laugh.

"Guess you picked the wrong century to time-travel into," said a very nervous Albert Einstein.

Max didn't actually speak to the most famous physicist in history. After all, Dr. Einstein passed away in 1955. But, from time to time, she did have imaginary conversations with him in her head. His voice was usually gentle, the way a kindly grandfather might sound (not that Max had ever had one of those).

But not today.

Today he sounded anxious.

"I am worried about you, Max," he said. "I developed so slowly that I did not begin to wonder about space and time until I was an adult. You? You might be a child but already you have to grapple with issues of time travel, doing good in the world, and now, global warming."

"They want to make me the brand image of a movement."

"Will they take your picture?"

"I guess."

"Oh, I hate my pictures," said Einstein. "Look at my face. If it weren't for this mustache, I'd look like a woman!"

That made Max grin. The Einstein in her head did that sometimes. It was one of the reasons she loved conversing with her imaginary mentor.

"Max, someone has to stop this global warming crisis," said Einstein, again sounding more worried and anxious than Max had ever heard him sound before. Then again, she was the one generating his voice. Maybe it was just a projection of how nervous and anxious she felt. Yes, fighting hunger and working for clean water had been huge undertakings. But this new fight? This was for the survival of the human race. Max figured the planet would be just fine after all the seas rose and the forests burned. Different, sure, but it would survive. Humans? Not so much.

"Maybe this is why you came here from 1921," Einstein continued.

"*If* that really happened," countered Max.

"Ah, yes. The almighty *if.*"

"They want to make me famous," said Max.

"It has its pluses and its minuses," said Einstein with a

casual shrug. "Fame can help you gain access to the powerful and mighty. It is how I was able to arrange an audience with President Roosevelt during World War Two. But, with fame, I fear I became more and more stupid, which of course is a very common phenomenon. But, in the end, the sculptor, the artist, the musician, the scientist work because they love their work. Fame and honor are secondary."

"I love doing good in this world," said Max. "Doing good feels good."

"So, then please keep it up, my young friend. The destiny of civilized humanity depends more than ever on the moral forces it is capable of generating."

The destiny of civilized humanity.

No wonder the Dr. Einstein in Max's head was freaking out.

That destiny was in jeopardy again. Just like it had been when Albert Einstein's theories were later used by others to help develop the atomic bomb.

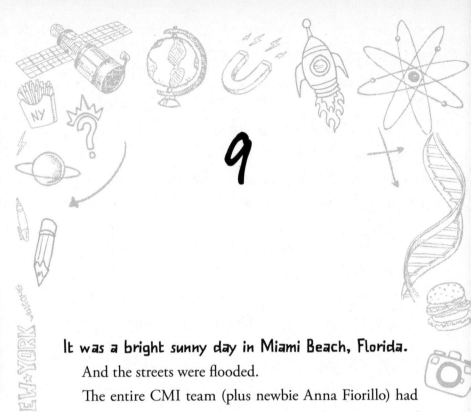

9

It was a bright sunny day in Miami Beach, Florida.

And the streets were flooded.

The entire CMI team (plus newbie Anna Fiorillo) had gathered in a street where water was gushing up out of storm grates. Leo wasn't with them. Water this deep was bad for his electronic components and battery packs.

Max looked around and realized something: Every single one of the kids on the CMI team had grown up facing an uncertain future because of the mistakes older generations had made.

Toma, the budding astrophysicist from China, was explaining king tides to the group.

Bright sunny day

This happens on a regular basis, whenever the moon and sun line up just so.

NASA estimates a global sea-level increase of three inches since 1992. NASA predicts sea level to be 14-26 inches higher by 2060.

I predict Miami will be great for Kayaking.

"A hurricane didn't do this," he said, sloshing through the ankle-high water. "A king tide—a higher-than-normal high tide—occurs when the sun and the moon line up just right, or, in this case, just wrong. King tides have always been a thing here in Miami Beach. Usually under a full or new moon. But they're getting worse because of sea-level rise brought on by climate change."

Klaus covered his mouth so he could cough out, "Hoax!"

Keeto, the cool computer-hacking kid from Oakland, was standing next to Klaus. "Hoax? Tell that to my soaked socks, dude."

"This flooding is not being caused by a 'rising sea,'" said Klaus, using air quotes. "It was created by sinking land. They used way too much sand in the landfill when they built up this area. You put heavy buildings on top of sand, the sand is going to sink."

Max studied Klaus. Could science, real science, ever convince a skeptic like him? Why did he feel compelled to come up with alternate explanations to inconvenient truths?

We'll never end this crisis, she thought, *until we convince all the Klauses in the world that it's really real!*

"Sinking land?" scoffed Siobhan. "Those glaciers we saw melting up in Greenland, all that ice turning into water?

It's like overfilling a bathtub, mate. That water has to go somewhere. Looks like it decided Miami would be nice this time of year."

Annika, the master of formal logic from Germany, pointed to some nearby construction. "As the waters continue to rise, efforts are underway to rebuild the roads and make everything higher. In effect, the city is saying, if the sea level is going to rise, our land level must also rise."

Keeto shook his head. "The rate of sea-level rise has tripled down here in just ten years. What are they going to do ten years from now? Build higher roads on top of their higher roads?"

"My point exactly," said Annika. "This is not the most logical solution."

"This is good, you guys," said Anna, who had her phone up and was videoing the CMI team's discussion. "Ben's gonna love this footage when he gets here. Max? You've been kind of quiet. I need a capper. Say something super smart and inspiring. Give me my sound bite."

"Those are typically nine seconds long," coached Max's friend Tisa, the biochemist from Kenya. Tisa and Max had really bonded on the group's first task in Africa. They bonded even more because they both hated taking the

CMI's intelligence tests. The two friends agreed with Albert Einstein, who once said, "It is in fact nothing short of a miracle that modern methods of instruction have not yet entirely strangled the holy curiosity of inquiry."

"Max?" Anna prompted again. "You're the group's face. Say something I can post on our socials. And maybe give your mop top a good shake right before you say it..."

Max hated speaking in public. She hated it even more when someone was jamming a camera in her face.

So she flicked out a hand to gesture at the rising water. "This, you know, stinks."

Everyone waited for her to say more.

She didn't.

"Oh-kay," said Anna. "You and I need to do a little media coaching, Max."

That's when Ben arrived on the scene in a chauffeured SUV.

He was talking on his phone as he stepped out of the vehicle and into the flooded street. Fortunately, he was wearing knee-high wader boots.

"That's, uh, great news. Thanks, you know, for setting it up. No, she'll be great. I promise. Max Einstein is a genius with a whole lot of, uh, important genius stuff to tell the world. Thanks again."

He ended the call.

"Uh, good news, guys," he said to the group, his eyes looking down at the water because, as Max knew, Ben sometimes had trouble looking people in the eye. "I mean, *this* isn't good news." He pointed at the water. "This is horrible. But I wanted you all to see it. In person. Same with the glaciers some of you visited. The earth's trying to tell us something. We need to move fast to fix this climate crisis. So, uh, that's why I'm glad Anna was able to set this thing up for you, Max."

Ben wiggled his phone.

"What thing?" asked Max.

Anna smiled. "You're going to address the United Nations General Assembly, girlfriend!"

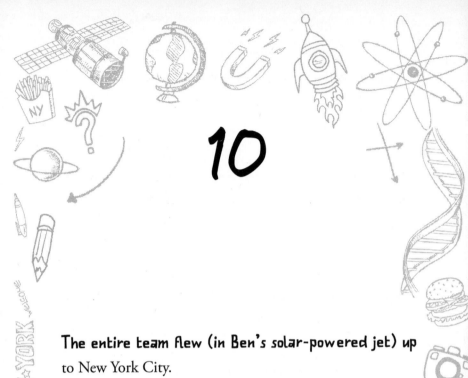

10

The entire team flew (in Ben's solar-powered jet) up to New York City.

"We'll brainstorm big, uh, planet-saving ideas to help Max prep her speech," Ben explained on the flight.

Max closed her eyes and wished she could disappear or time-travel to some other wrinkle on the time-space continuum.

"We want big, BIG ideas," said the marketing maven, Anna Fiorillo. "Something with sizzle that's guaranteed to grab eyeballs."

Klaus raised his hand. "Am I the only one on this airplane who thinks we're wasting our time? There are so many other big issues we could deal with. Real issues, like global poverty. Climate change is such a huge hoax. The earth is just doing what it does. Temperatures go up and then they go down. Sea levels rise and then they recede. This planet is far more powerful and responsive than the humans living on its surface and will change itself when the time is right."

"You're joking," said Keeto. "Right?"

"No, I think you people are the joke. I don't believe any of the science behind this conspiracy of gloom and doom."

"Well," said Keeto, "let me drop a little Neil deGrasse Tyson on you, Klaus. 'The good thing about science is that it's true whether or not you believe in it.'"

When the jet landed at a private airfield in New Jersey, Max was mobbed by a team of reporters and a gaggle of cameras.

"I gave them a tip that you might be arriving today," whispered Anna.

"Tell us more about how you busted the Corp in West Virginia, Max!" shouted a reporter. "Was that United States senator really involved?"

"What are you going to tell the United Nations?" yelled another.

"Are you really related to Albert Einstein?" asked a third. "Are you his great-great-granddaughter or something?"

Max wanted to turn around and dash back up the airstairs so she could hide in the solar jet's bathroom. But Anna grabbed her gently by the elbow and edged her forward.

"Just smile," Anna whispered through tight teeth.

Max smiled. Sort of. It was more like a quivering grimace.

"Ms. Einstein is preparing a major address for the entire world in two days," Anna told the cameras. "What she and her friends did to fight world hunger they'll soon be doing in the fight against global warming. She can't really discuss her remarks right now. But—rest assured—change is coming. Stand by for something big. No, let me rephrase that. Stand by for something HUGE!"

The clutch of reporters let out a collective *whoo* of admiration for the young YouTube star's brash promise.

Max sighed. She had to say something to tamp down the wild expectations Anna had just amped up.

"We just want to do good in the world," Max said, humbly. "Doing good feels good."

So many cameras flashed in her face, Max started seeing spots.

Finally, a fleet of electric vehicles arrived to whisk Ben

and his CMI crew into New York City where he'd rented an entire floor in a high-rise hotel at One UN Plaza. It was the closest hotel to the United Nations, where Max was scheduled to speak in two days.

If she didn't die during a panic attack first.

"Don't worry, Max," said Anna, when the group arrived at their hotel. "The whole team is going to meet in an hour to toss around some more global warming solutions. Except Klaus. He doesn't think there's a problem, so..."

Max nodded but didn't say anything. She felt queasy. The butterflies in her stomach had butterflies in their stomachs. She did not want to stand up at a marble podium and address the representatives of 193 sovereign states that made up the United Nations General Assembly. Talk about *public* speaking. The whole world would be watching.

"Just go to your room and chill for a little," suggested Anna, "then come down to our conference room ready to discuss the awesome ideas from the best and brightest young brains in the world—including yours, of course. Your speech will practically write itself."

Max hurried across the lobby and caught the next elevator.

She raced up to her room, all the while wishing the elevator had a button that could take her back to 1921.

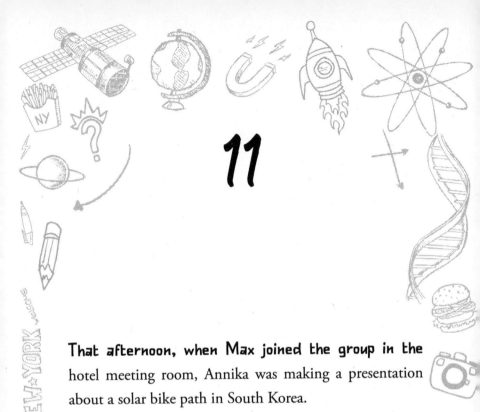

11

That afternoon, when Max joined the group in the hotel meeting room, Annika was making a presentation about a solar bike path in South Korea.

"This is one of the most elegant alternative-energy solutions I have ever seen," she said, pointing to the screen behind her. Cars were whizzing along what looked like the South Korean version of an interstate highway. Three lanes of traffic were heading one way; three lanes of traffic were heading the other. In the median dividing the highway was a long strip of angled, dark-gray solar panels. "That's twenty miles of solar panels, set up to provide a canopy to protect the bike lane from the elements."

"Whoa," said Keeto. "There's a bike lane underneath all those solar cells?"

"Yes," said Annika. "And, of course, alternative forms of transportation, such as bicycles, are another way to reduce our carbon footprint. The less carbon we throw up into the atmosphere, the more we reduce the greenhouse effect."

"I like it," said Ben, seated at the head of the long conference table.

This was new for Ben. Max was used to the Change Makers Institute's mysterious young benefactor hiding in the shadows. Staying out of the day-to-day activities of the group. Maybe the challenge and pressure of trying to solve global warming was forcing him to climb out of his comfort zone.

"But..."

Annika's face dropped. Nobody liked hearing that particular sentence. *I like it, but...*

"What's your *but*, Ben?" asked Anna, which, of course, made Keeto and Toma snicker.

Ben sighed. "It's already been, you know, done. If we repeat what South Korea did in some other location, no one will really notice or pay attention."

"If it's a smart idea, who bloomin' cares if anybody notices?" said Siobhan. "Since when are we in this for the publicity?"

"Since it's what you need," said Anna, the publicity expert. "The attention you inadvertently generated shutting down the Corp in West Virginia is what guaranteed that they went out of business and won't be coming back. Just doing good for the sake of doing good is like peeing your pants in a dark suit."

The boys giggled again. Well, Keeto and Toma. Not Vihaan. He seemed to be blushing a little.

"Excuse me?" said Annika, shocked.

"Peeing your pants in a dark suit?" said Siobhan.

"What's that supposed to mean?" asked Tisa.

Anna shrugged. "You get a nice warm feeling but nobody else notices. If we want the world to change its ways, first we have to do something dramatic to make people sit up and take notice. We have to throw a pie in their face and, once we have their attention, tell them something smart."

More ideas about how to solve global warming were tossed around the room. Some were definitely pretty wild.

"Keep worms in the kitchen!" said Tisa. "They can turn food scraps into compost to be used in gardens. Organic waste does not decompose in the dark, low-oxygen conditions of municipal landfills. Instead, it produces methane, a greenhouse gas more potent than carbon dioxide."

"You want big?" said Keeto. "How about this: We give the earth some sunscreen! We put a ring of sunlight-scattering particles or tiny satellites in orbit around the equator. The ring blocks some of the solar radiation trying to bake the surface just like sunscreen protects your skin."

Oh-kay, thought Max. *That was definitely a big idea. Practical? Not so much.*

There was talk about weatherizing homes. Investing in energy-efficient appliances. Reducing water waste. Wasting less food. Eating less meat. Buying better light bulbs. Unplugging video consoles when they weren't in use.

Around four p.m., Ben called for a break.

"Let's knock off for thirty minutes. And then come back and, uh, you know, wow me."

"Blow his socks off," added Anna. "Go big or go home!"

Max got up with everybody else.

"I need to head up to my room," she told Ben.

"Is that where you keep the big ideas?" asked Anna with a wink.

Max smiled. "Something like that."

Max headed to the elevator. No one else got on with her.

That was a good thing. Because she wasn't going up to her room.

She went down to the lobby and then outside for a walk.

Because that's when you get the big ideas. When you weren't trying to force them. You did something else—you walked the dog or did the dishes—and, before you knew it, an idea bubbled up.

Hopefully.

Because Max still had no idea what she was going to say in her address to the United Nations.

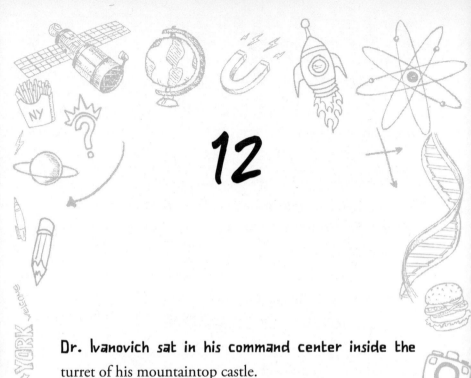

12

Dr. Ivanovich sat in his command center inside the turret of his mountaintop castle.

He was rolling the pair of diamonds between his hands as he contemplated his next move against Max Einstein and all who would dare stop him.

Their minds would be no match for his.

Satellite feeds from international news networks filled the two dozen video monitors mounted on the castle's damp stone walls.

And Max Einstein was on every single screen.

"I see our young friend has arrived in New York City to great fanfare," he said to his guest.

"She was never my friend," replied Tari Kaplan. "She was the benefactor's favorite, not mine. She was terrible at taking written exams..."

"And these other children with her, they are the entire Change Makers team?"

"Yes," said Ms. Kaplan. "My friend—and accomplice—the brilliant young botanist Hana is no longer with them. She was unceremoniously sent home to Japan."

"Meanwhile," said the cunning doctor, "you were unceremoniously sent to jail."

Ms. Kaplan, always a proud woman, lowered her head in shame. "I am grateful for your efforts in gaining my release."

"You mean you are grateful for my ten million dollars in bail money. I hope you will prove a worthwhile investment, Ms. Kaplan. I'm sure the American authorities would appreciate any and all information concerning your whereabouts..."

"There," she said, pointing at the screen, hoping to prove her worth to Dr. Ivanovich and the Fossils. "That boy there. That's Benjamin Abercrombie. He's their billionaire backer. However..."

"What?"

"I don't see Charl or Isabl. Not on any of the news feeds.

Typically, they are present but attempting to blend into the background..."

"And who, pray tell, are Charl and Isabl?"

"The CMI's muscle. Their crack security squad. Both Charl and Isabl are incredibly skilled special forces operatives and weapons experts. They're the ones who orchestrated the humiliating capture of Professor Von Hinkle and myself."

Dr. Ivanovich clacked his diamonds together a little faster. "*Zdorovo.* Excellent. Thank you for that intelligence, Ms. Kaplan. It seems you are, indeed, earning your keep."

"It also seems that Max Einstein is less protected than she has been in the past," said Kaplan. "Plus, the CMI used to operate in secret. They never splashed themselves all over the news like this. But now, I sense they have changed direction, hoping to generate as much buzz as they can with this grand entrance into New York City and the showcase of an address to the United Nations."

Dr. Ivanovich narrowed his eyes. "I suspect their success against the Corp has emboldened this young band of troublemakers and their financial backer."

Ms. Kaplan nodded. "I suspect you are correct, Dr. Ivanovich."

The doctor quit his nervous fidgeting with the two diamonds. A sickly smile curled across his lips, inching up his thick mustache. "Let us hope they continue to generate such extraordinary media coverage during the rest of their visit. It will make it that much easier for our minions to track down and eliminate Max Einstein."

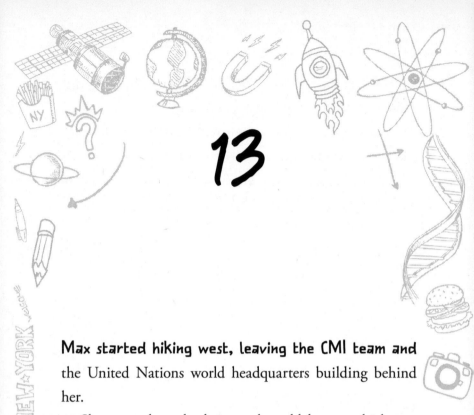

13

Max started hiking west, leaving the CMI team and the United Nations world headquarters building behind her.

She wanted to check in on her old home, which was way over on the other side of Manhattan Island near the Hudson River. Max figured it would take her forty-nine minutes to hike the 2.2 miles, giving her plenty of time to daydream.

What could she possibly say to the General Assembly of the United Nations that would help set the world on a course to, finally, deal with the crisis of global warming?

Should she tell everybody to keep worms in their kitchen and compost their organic waste?

Should she talk about bike lanes sheltered under solar panels?

Or maybe she could borrow a few lines from Albert Einstein, who addressed the UN through an open letter in October of 1947. He wrote, "We are caught in a situation in which every citizen of every country, his children, and his life's work, are threatened by the terrible insecurity which reigns in our world today."

In 1947, it was the atomic bomb.

Today, it was global warming.

Either one, if left unchecked, could eliminate human life from the face of the planet.

But Max wondered if Albert Einstein would be a global warming skeptic, like her CMI teammate Klaus.

"Global warming alarmists always say 'ninety-seven percent of scientists' support them," Klaus had said to Max. "But remember the attack on your dear professor in that book called *A Hundred Scientists Against Einstein,* which was published in Germany in 1931."

When confronted with one hundred scientists lined up

against him, Einstein had said, "If I were wrong, then one would have been enough!"

In other words, Klaus didn't care if 97 percent of the world's scientists thought global warming was real because he knew they were all wrong.

Max wasn't sure where Einstein would stand on the issue of global warming. Maybe he'd be too busy trying to understand and explain the entire cosmos to worry about one planet whirling around inside it.

She wished she could ask him.

Max arrived at "the Stables," a brand-new apartment complex for low-income renters. It used to be a stable for Central Park carriage horses. That's when Max and several other homeless people used to "squat" rent-free on the vacant floors above the horse stalls. After the first CMI adventure, Ben Abercrombie bought the dilapidated old building, gutted it, renovated it, and turned the whole place into affordable housing for all of Max's formerly homeless friends.

One of those old friends, Mr. Kennedy, was on the sidewalk in front of the building, staring under the raised hood of a yellow taxi. The cabbie was staring with him. So was Mrs. Rabinowitz, another one of Max's former neighbors.

She was clutching a brown grocery sack to her chest and shaking her head. There was a young girl, maybe five years old, standing next to her.

"That engine's dead," said Mrs. Rabinowitz.

"It's not dead," said Mr. Kennedy, who always sounded gruff and ornery, even though he was really just a gray-haired ol' teddy bear. "It's just a leaky radiator."

"But my garage is all the way out in Queens," said the cabbie.

Max walked up the sidewalk and joined the group. "Hi, guys."

"Max?" said Mr. Kennedy. "What're you doing here?"

"Just thought I'd drop by the old 'hood."

"She's going to be addressing the United Nations in two days," said Mrs. Rabinowitz. "Aren't you, Max?"

The cabdriver laughed. "Really? How old are you, kid?"

"Twelve," said Max.

"Well, Maxine," said Mr. Kennedy, who thought Mrs. Rabinowitz was just spouting another one of her flaky fantasies, "you couldn't do any worse than all the grown-ups they've got running that place."

"Ain't that the truth," said the cabbie.

"Max?" said Mrs. Rabinowitz. "I want you to meet my

grandniece, Shaila Kiriluk. She's five and a half and collects the stickers off fruits. She's always wanted to see New York City but, well, I never had a place nice enough for her to stay. Not until you and your friend Benjamin fixed up the stables."

The young girl thrust out her hand. "Hi. I'm Shaila."

"Hi. I'm Max. Let's see if we can help out this cabbie, okay?"

"Okay."

Max leaned in and checked out the cab's engine.

"Mrs. Rabinowitz? Could I buy a couple eggs from you?" She handed her a dollar. "Two would do."

"Well, all right, dear…"

Mrs. Rabinowitz took the money and fished two eggs out of the cardboard carton riding at the top of her grocery sack.

"Planning a late breakfast?" she asked.

Max smiled. "No, ma'am." She turned to the cabdriver. "I can temporarily fix your radiator leak, sir."

"With eggs?" said the skeptical cabbie.

Max nodded and pointed at a hissing spot on the radiator. "Is that the leak?"

"Yep," said Mr. Kennedy.

Max cracked open an egg then rocked the shells back and forth to separate the white from the yolk. She let the clear liquid drizzle down onto the leaky spot.

"What the..." said the cabbie.

"This should patch things up," explained Max. "You see, heat from your radiator will cook the egg whites while pressure will force the cooked egg solids into any holes to plug them up. This hack should hold long enough for you to drive your car to that garage in Queens for repairs."

"Well, I'll be..." said the cabbie as his radiator quit hissing steam.

"That's why we call her Max Einstein," said Mr. Kennedy with a big laugh. "Smartest kid I ever met."

"She's a genius!" added the five-year-old, Shaila.

Now a stranger came up the sidewalk.

A man in his midtwenties.

"You're Max Einstein?" said the young man.

He was dressed in a snow camo T-shirt and matching baggy pants. He was also carrying a small gym bag.

"I can't believe I just bumped into you on the streets. This is my lucky day."

The man bent down to unzip his bag.

Max was ready to run.

Because the guy in the snow camo clothes looked very similar to the guys who had chased Max and Siobhan across the slick surface of that melting glacier up in Greenland.

14

Max's heart raced as she swiveled on her heels.

She needed to run!

But the man in the snow camo was fast. He bent over, zipped open his gym bag, and whipped out...

...a copy of that morning's tabloid newspaper.

"Can I get your autograph?" he asked.

Max's face was on the front page under a banner head-line screaming in big block letters: **THE EARTH IS ON FIRE, BUT SO IS MAX!**

"Well, look at that," said Mr. Kennedy, reading the headline. "You really are gonna talk to the UN."

Max nodded. "Day after tomorrow."

"I'm a big fan, Ms. Einstein," said the guy in the white camo clothes that he probably just wore because he thought they made him look cool. He held out a pen.

Max took it and scrawled her signature across the front page of the newspaper.

"What're you gonna say in your speech?" the eager fan asked.

Max had to laugh. "Good question. I better head back to the hotel and work on it."

"Oh, yes," said Mrs. Rabinowitz. "When speaking in public, preparation is key. Like Ben Franklin said, failing to prepare is preparing to fail."

Little Shaila gave that a wink.

Max laughed. Who knew Mrs. Rabinowitz could be so pithy? Or that her grandniece could be so cute.

Max said her good-byes to her old and new friends and wandered back east, taking her time, taking in some of her old familiar haunts. The Mee Noodle Shop was still there on Ninth Avenue and 53rd Street. Max sniffed the delicious aroma of boiled dumplings and moo goo gai pan and fried rice wafting out the front door as delivery people bustled to their bikes, toting heavy brown sacks of food. Max and the owner of the noodle shop, Mr. Lin, had always been friends. From time to time when she lived above the stables, Max would be the one hopping on a bicycle to do dinner rush deliveries. She'd only been eleven, so her paycheck always came in a cardboard take-out container: free food. (She also got to keep her tips!)

Max was smiling, admiring the steamy window of the noodle shop, when she gasped. In the glass reflection, she saw, of course, herself, and someone standing behind her. A flickering, ghosting image of a slump-shouldered man with a tangle of wild white hair and a bushy mustache. She whirled around.

It was Professor Einstein.

Not the one she talked to in her head. *The real deal.*

But this Einstein image kept fading in and out like an antique video clip on a brittle tape that had degraded over time and lost most of its magnetic signal. Max wondered if the image was, somehow, straddling the time-space continuum. One foot in the present, another in the past.

"Dr. Einstein?" Max gulped, trying to catch her breath.

"Hello, Dorothy," said Einstein, his face warbling in and out of focus.

Dorothy. If the stories were true, that was the name of the toddler sent forward into the future by a married couple of young genius professors who were using their special relativity time machine.

No one called Max Dorothy.

Except Professor McKenna from Princeton University who had been doing research on what might've happened in the house that Max had labeled Tardis House because it had a time machine in its basement. The Einstein inside her head always called her Max.

"Your parents, Dorothy..." said Einstein. "Your parents..." His image became a flashing, fluttering, shivering loop.

And then it was gone.

Oh-kay, thought Max. *Somebody's been smelling too much sweet-and-sour Chinese food.* The ginger and soy sauce were playing tricks on her mind. She was seeing things.

Or was she?

Because there was a young boy standing on the sidewalk, a Tootsie Pop frozen in mid-lick. And he, like Max, was gawking at the empty space where Dr. Albert Einstein had (maybe) just momentarily materialized before he disappeared.

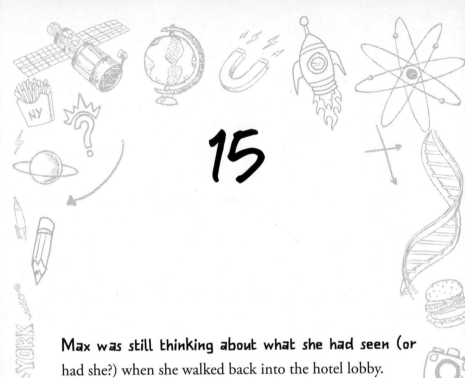

15

Max was still thinking about what she had seen (or had she?) when she walked back into the hotel lobby.

"Where have you been?" demanded Anna Sophia Fiorillo. "You've been gone for hours."

"I, um, needed to clear my head."

"You look like you've just seen a ghost."

Because maybe I did.

"I'm fine," Max said with a weak smile. Anna Fiorillo was a whiz kid when it came to marketing. Probably not so much on the whole Einsteinian concept of time travel, which, of course, would be based on his study of time in relation to the speed of light.

"Look," said Anna, "your speech is the day after tomorrow. A lot is riding on it. Maybe everything."

"Yeah," said Max, without adding "don't remind me."

"How are you in front of a huge audience?"

Max arched her eyebrows. "Petrified. Basically."

"Understandable," said Anna. "You're a thinker and a doer. Not a talker. Come on."

"Where are we going?"

"The conference room. Let me give you a few pointers about public speaking."

"Is everybody else still in there?" Max could feel her internal panic alarms ringing.

"Nope. They went to dinner. Klaus wanted to try New York's famous sausage and pepper sandwiches. This will just be you and me."

Phew. "Thank you!"

Max and Anna went into the empty meeting room.

"So, how far along are you on your speech?" asked Anna.

"Not very," said Max. "I haven't written a single word."

"That's okay. You've got the rest of the night and all of tomorrow. I think your fear of speaking in public might be holding you back from writing down all the great things you have to say...because you're going to have to say them in front of an audience."

Max nodded. Anna Fiorillo was part cheerleader, part psychiatrist.

"Okay, here are my top tips. First, talk about what you know. That way, your passion for the topic will be felt by the audience. When you're done writing, practice speaking. And after you practice, practice some more. Visit the room where you'll be giving the speech. Okay, you can't actually do that. But you can study it. Google 'Speeches, General Assembly, United Nations.' You'll have a better idea of what you're stepping into before you step into it."

Max was making mental notes. Letting it all soak in.

"Concentrate on your message and, while you're at it, make sure you only have *one* main message. Tie everything back to that single theme. Avoid filler words like 'basically,' 'well,' and 'um.' This is the U-N. They don't want to hear you saying U-M all the time."

"Got it," said Max.

"Find a friendly face in the crowd," coached Anna. "For instance, me. Pretend you're speaking to just that one person."

"Okay."

"Because that's what you're doing right now, Max. You're talking to me."

"I know."

"And you're doing great. So, on speech day, do the same thing. Pretend all those other people aren't even in the room. I guess that's my number one tip, Max. Talk. Don't present. Back in 1863, a guy named Edward Everett, who was considered the greatest orator of his day, gave a two-hour speech at the Gettysburg battlefield in Pennsylvania. But we remember the other guy who spoke that day. Abraham Lincoln. The one who *talked* for two minutes."

"Thanks, Anna. You're good at this stuff."

Someone tapped on the conference room door.

"Come in," said Anna, after Max nodded that it was okay.

Leo, the automaton, strode into the room. He'd been in Klaus's room "monitoring the security situation in the absence of Charl and Isabl," as he put it.

"I hate to interrupt," said Leo.

"That's okay," said Max. "Anna was just helping me work on my speech."

"Be sure to stand up straight, Max," said Leo. "Greet your audience. Perhaps open with a joke. And smile."

"Riiiight," said Max. It seemed that everybody, human or android, knew more about public speaking than Max.

"What's up?" asked Anna.

"Ms. Tari Kaplan is unaccounted for," said Leo.

"Excuse me?" said Max.

"Her bail was posted, she was released from jail, but she did not show up for her scheduled court appearance today. She is, as they say, in the wind. A fugitive from justice. A bail jumper. She is also, in my estimation, a very serious security threat. Perhaps you should reconsider addressing the United Nations."

Oh-kay.

This was a lot.

I have to write a speech. I have to recite it. In front of dignitaries representing the whole entire world.

And, I have to worry about Ms. Kaplan wreaking her revenge.

She turned to the robot.

"Thanks for the heads-up, Leo, but I have to do this. As scheduled. Because guess what? The world's running out of time."

16

On the morning of the big day, Max watched a little TV news while she ate her breakfast.

She, unlike her hero Albert Einstein, had cereal and a banana. Einstein liked fried eggs, honey, and mushrooms for breakfast. Yeah. Slimy mushrooms. Gross. Even smothered with honey.

Max hoped Klaus was watching the same channel she was. Because she'd defy him to remain a climate change denier after seeing the news network's "special weather update." Death Valley had registered temperatures over 130 degrees. California had wildfires that roared through more than one million acres. Oregon and Washington

State were blazing, too. Two separate hurricanes churned across the Gulf of Mexico at the same time. And this was all happening with just a one-degree Celsius increase in average temps worldwide.

What would happen when that became a two-degree increase?

Max realized she didn't have the luxury of being nervous about giving a speech in front of the UN. She had to deliver some kind of wake-up call to the world before it was too late. If it wasn't too late already.

Someone knocked on her hotel room door.

It was Anna.

"You ready to stroll over?" she asked.

"Just about."

"Great. I'll go with you. We can do some pre-speech interviews and press availabilities on the way. Build up suspense and anticipation for your major address."

"Um, if it's okay with you, Anna, I'd rather walk over to the UN alone." She tapped her head. "It'll give me time to rehearse once more."

Anna sighed. "Okay. Fine. If that's what you need to do. But wear a ski cap or a baseball cap or, I don't know, a shower cap. Something to hide your trademark flaming-red curls.

If you don't, you'll be mobbed before you reach the security gates."

"Good idea. I'll wear a Yankees hat."

"Awesome. And put on some sunglasses, too. I'll meet you at the security check-in, escort you to the greenroom. That's where you'll wait before you speak."

Thirty minutes later, with her hair jammed up inside a souvenir baseball cap the hotel sold in its gift shop, Max shuffled out of the lobby and made her way over to the United Nations building, which was, basically, right across the street.

She paused for a second to admire the UN's *Non-Violence* sculpture, a giant bronze replica of a .357 Magnum revolver with its muzzle tied into a knot. It was originally created as a memorial tribute to the late John Lennon by his Swedish friend the artist Carl Fredrik Reuterswärd. It's the first artwork visitors see when they approach the outdoor plaza at the UN entrance at 46th Street and First Avenue.

It, of course, symbolizes the United Nations' role in working for peaceful solutions to world problems.

"Violence may at times have quickly cleared away an obstruction," said the voice of Einstein in her head, "but it has never proved itself to be creative."

"And now the violence is coming from Mother Nature," said Max. Out loud. Even though the Einstein she was conversing with was the one in her head, not the one she thought she saw outside the noodle shop. "Of course, she's getting a ton of help from all of us humans."

"Indeed," said Einstein. "But I have faith in you, Max, and all those your age. I hope that your generation will someday put mine to shame."

"You wrote that in a letter to the schoolchildren of Japan," said Max.

A pair of tourists was staring at her. Not because they recognized her. Because she was talking to herself.

She tapped her ear as if to indicate that she were on a phone call (even though she wasn't wearing earbuds).

"You also wrote an open letter to the UN in 1947," said Max.

Now more people were gawping at her. Some had confused looks on their faces as if to say, "I wasn't even born in 1947."

"Yes," replied her internal Einstein. "I was attempting to do what you are attempting to do. To implore the nations of the world to break the vicious circle that threatens the

continued existence of mankind as no other situation in human history has ever done."

Max reached the security gates. Anna was there waiting for her.

So was everybody else. Even Klaus.

"You can do this, Max!" shouted Keeto.

"You're goin' to be bloomin' awesome!" added Siobhan.

"I believe in you," shouted Klaus. "Just not your science."

Max had a slight lump in her throat. She'd never really had a family. She'd been an orphan and had lived on the streets. But now? She had a whole bunch of brothers and sisters—the entire CMI team! And they were all cheering her on.

17

Max had never felt so small.

For the audience to see her, she had to stand on a wooden box behind the giant stone podium with double microphones set up in front of a swirled-green marble wall. It was the same spot where presidents and prime ministers and other dignitaries had addressed the General Assembly of the United Nations for decades.

It looked like all 1,800 seats in the cavernous auditorium were filled. Her words were about to be simultaneously translated so they could be heard in all six official languages of the UN: Arabic, Chinese, English, French, Russian, and Spanish.

She took a deep breath and pretended she was talking to just one person, not all 1,800 of them. She tried to find Anna in the crowd but the lights shining straight into her eyes were too bright. So she focused on a silhouette at the back of the room. A stranger. Hopefully, a friendly stranger.

She took in a deep, calming breath and began.

"A few years ago, you heard from one of my heroes, Greta Thunberg, the young environmental activist from Sweden. She said, 'I shouldn't be up here. I should be back in school on the other side of the ocean. Yet, you all come to us young people for hope. How dare you!'

"Perhaps what Greta told you that day bears repeating. That people are suffering. That people are dying. That entire ecosystems are collapsing. That we are in the beginning of a mass extinction—an extinction that could include all of humanity.

"As you undoubtedly remember, Greta pointed out in no uncertain terms that science about climate change has been crystal clear for more than thirty years. But what you might not remember is what one of my other heroes, Professor Albert Einstein, told you, the General Assembly of the United Nations, in an open letter nearly a century ago, all the way back in October 1947. He wrote about the threat of global destruction that *could* be brought on by the atomic bomb. Well, now we are faced with a new threat of global destruction that *will* be brought on by climate change if we don't change our ways.

"Perhaps this destruction isn't as instantaneous and, therefore, not as dramatic or frightening as someone pushing a button and destroying the entire planet by showering it with atomic bombs. But, make no mistake about it, the threat we face today is just as terrifying. For, as Einstein wrote, 'We are caught in a situation in which every citizen of every country, their children, their life's work, are threatened by the terrible insecurity which reigns in our world today.' Back then, it was the atomic bomb. Today, we have another looming threat—the climate crisis brought on by global warming. In 1947, Dr. Einstein looked to you, the United Nations. He urged you to serve the single-minded goal of guaranteeing the 'security, tranquility, and welfare' of the world.

"Well, today, I, like Greta Thunberg and so many others before me, urge you to do the same. To guarantee the welfare of the entire world by eliminating this threat to our very existence. To do whatever it takes to reverse our current course. If we do not act, and act fast, the world as we know it will be in grave danger. There will be more once-in-five-hundred-years floods, more wildfires, more drought, famine, and climate refugees. The seas will rise, coastlines will be redrawn, farming will suffer, forest fires will rage out of control, and species of fish and animals will disappear. As your own secretary general pointed out, climate change is moving faster than we are.

"But, all is not gloom and doom. If we, as a world of united nations, act now, we have hope. Did you know that our generous sun already sends us more energy every single hour than the whole world uses each year? We just have to use our brains to harness it.

"Renewable energy is thriving. A recent study predicts that clean energy technologies have become so cost effective they will, if we let them, replace fossil fuels as our main energy source within the next twenty years!

"The political winds are shifting around this topic, too. And young people, like me, Greta Thunberg, and millions of others, are on the march because the future is where we'll spend most of our time. All around the globe, kids are angry that the adults are not acting like, well, adults. As Thunberg put it, 'We can no longer save the world by playing by the rules because the rules have to be changed!' "

Max paused and tried to, somehow, lock eyes with the whole auditorium.

"Look," she said, "we all know that it is right to save the future. It's not easy, but it *is* right. So let's all work together and do the right thing. Let's save the one and only thing every single nation on the face of the earth shares. Our planet. Thank you."

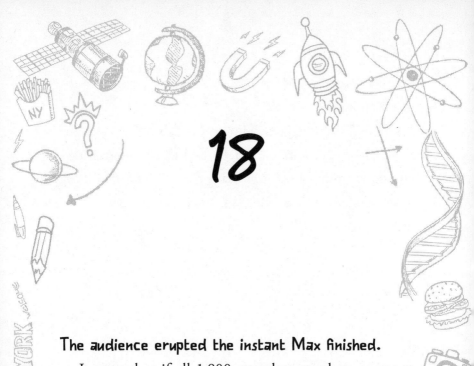

18

The audience erupted the instant Max finished.

It seemed as if all 1,800 attendees stood up as one to give Max a rousing ovation. Their cheers echoed off the high ceiling and rang off the marble-covered walls.

The lights came up in the auditorium and Max could see her CMI friends in a clump of seats near the back of the room, behind the assembled dignitaries. Keeto was *woo-hoo*ing. Siobhan was doing two-fingered whistles. Her friends were cheering louder than anybody.

Well, everybody except Klaus. He was still seated and shaking his head. He was also fidgeting with his phone in his lap. Max could tell it would take a lot more than one

stirring speech to convince Klaus (and all the other climate change deniers in the world) that their lives and the lives of the entire human race were in grave danger.

Max made her way off the speaking platform and down into the crowd. She shook hands and posed for a few selfies.

"Well done, young lady," said a man with a thick Russian accent. He also had a wild head of unkempt black hair and a bushy black mustache. Max grinned a little. The Russian man reminded her of a younger, wilder-eyed version of Albert Einstein. The man was rolling something around in his closed fist. Whatever it was, it made clicking and clacking noises.

"Thank you," said Max.

"I am Dr. Olezka Ivanovich. I am here as a guest of Vasily Alekseevich Nebenzya—Russia's Permanent Representative to the United Nations." Now the man bowed slightly. "I came, specifically, to hear you, Max Einstein. I have followed your, shall we say, 'global adventures' with great interest. It is a very great honor to finally meet you and, of course, to hear you speak."

"Thank you," said Max. "It is a very great honor to meet you as well." Max echoed the Russian's remarks in an attempt to sound diplomatic. It seemed to be the thing to do in a crowd of diplomats. "Now, if you will excuse me, I need to rejoin my group."

"Ah, yes," said Dr. Ivanovich. "The Change Makers Institute. Have Charl and Isabl rejoined the team?"

That startled Max.

"Excuse me?" she said. This seemingly innocent conversation had just taken a strange turn. How did this Dr. Ivanovich know about Charl and Isabl, the special forces operatives that typically served as the CMI's security detail during field operations?

The two highly skilled ex-military personnel weren't in New York with the team. They hadn't been in Miami or Greenland, either. Probably because, with the Corp out of business, the CMI's threat level had been (theoretically) reduced to zero.

Max squinted hard and studied Dr. Ivanovich's coal-black eyes. "How do you know about Charl and Isabl?"

Dr. Ivanovich shrugged. "I am, as I said, a big, big fan of the Change Makers Institute. I know all the players. All the history. Ah, I see Benjamin Franklin Abercrombie is here in the audience." He gestured with his head to the back of the auditorium. "Kindly give your benefactor my warmest regards."

"Does he know you?"

"No. But, perhaps, one day, he will. Enjoy the rest of your time here in New York City, Maxine."

Max nodded and backed away from the increasingly creepy Russian, who'd turned to chat with some other members of the Russian delegation. She heard one of the men laugh and say, *"Rozygrysh!"*

"Whoa, watch where you're going, Max."

It was Anna. Max had almost bumped into her as she backed up with her eyes fixed on the chuckling Russians.

"You did great up there," said Anna. "You didn't give a speech. You talked. Straight from the heart. Plus, the camera loves you. I want to have you sit down with a few of the networks, chat with some international correspondents. But, unfortunately, Ben won't let me."

"Why not?"

"There's somebody he wants you to meet. Right away. Back at the hotel."

"Who?"

Now Anna shrugged. "Not sure. He just told me it's a new member of the team. Someone to replace Hana."

19

It was another Russian.

A young guy named Alexei, but he was nowhere near as creepy as Dr. Ivanovich. In fact, Alexei was stunningly handsome with soft blond hair and intense blue eyes. There was something innocent and boyish about his face.

"Um, hello," said Max when they met in a hotel conference room. "So, uh, you're a botanist?"

Alexei grinned. Both of his cheeks dimpled when he did.

"No." He raised an eyebrow playfully. "Sorry. Are you having trouble with your house plants?"

Alexei had just the faintest hint of a Russian accent.

"No," said Max, feeling slightly embarrassed. "I don't actually have any house plants. It's just that they, uh, told me you were replacing Hana..."

"Ah, Hana. The mole. Do you need a new one?" Alexei asked with a very winning smile. "Someone to betray you? Not that all botanists are moles, mind you. In fact, I understand that many botanists dedicate their lives to defeating the burrowing rodents destroying their gardens from below..."

Max started laughing. "Okay, okay. So what is your field of expertise if it's not botany?"

"Nothing remotely scientific."

"Huh?"

That answer didn't make sense. The Change Maker kids had all been recruited for their genius-level problem-solving expertise in various scientific fields. Geoscience. Computer science. Astrophysics. Quantum physics. Biochemistry. Formal logic. They were all laser focused on science, technology, engineering, and math.

"I'm more of a humanist," Alexei explained. "I can speak seven different languages. I can read books written in fourteen. I'm also a writer."

"In which language?"

Alexei smiled again. "Most of them."

"Do you understand Russian?"

"*Da,*" said Alexei, using the Russian word for "yes."

"So, what does *rozygrysh* mean?"

"Hoax."

Max nodded. She now understood that Dr. Ivanovich had been totally leading her on with his fawning compliments. He didn't care about global warming. He and his snickering friends thought climate change was a "rozygrysh." A hoax. They were on Team Klaus.

"I'm a storyteller, Max," said Alexei. "That's why Ben invited me to join your team. Do you know why the young environmental protestors like Greta Thunberg have been so successful?"

Max shook her head because she really wanted to hear whatever Alexei might say next.

"Because they stopped telling stories about polar bears stranded on chunks of floating ice and started telling tales that bring the climate crisis home. Their message isn't about saving the rain forest or the whales. It's about floods sweeping away a neighbor's farmland and livelihood. About the wildfires burning in their backyards. About cherished family photographs being destroyed when muddy floodwaters swirl through a small town. They also talk about how disappointed they are in their parents and grandparents for kicking this can of ecological disaster down to the next generation. But, as you pointed out in your speech..."

Max blushed a little. "You saw that?"

Alexei nodded. "It was streaming live. I watched it on my phone. And, Max?"

Max swallowed a little. "Yes."

"You're quite good. Dynamic. And, as you said, all is not gloom and doom. We need to tell those positive stories. To highlight brilliant solutions. For instance, in Luxembourg, they've made all public transportation free for everybody. The free rides are great, of course. I mean, who doesn't like a free ride? But free buses and trains mean fewer cars on the street. That'll cut down on Luxembourg's greenhouse gas emissions. The more we write and talk about the ability to build a greener future, the more we give folks hope, the more likely we are to get to that future."

Max nodded. She could listen to Alexei talk all day.

"You should be the spokesperson," she told him. "Not me."

Alexei shook his head. "Sorry. I'm just here to help, Max. You're the face of this movement. I don't really like being in the spotlight..."

Welcome to the club, thought Max.

"But," said Alexei, "I can help you find and shape stories to drive your message home."

"In all those different languages."

Alexei nodded. "If that's what it takes."

Max's cell phone buzzed. So did Alexei's.

They both checked their screens.

It was a text from Ben.

CMI TEAM:

We have our next project.

Please report immediately to the large conference room.

This is going to be BIG!

PART TWO

Go Big or Stay Home

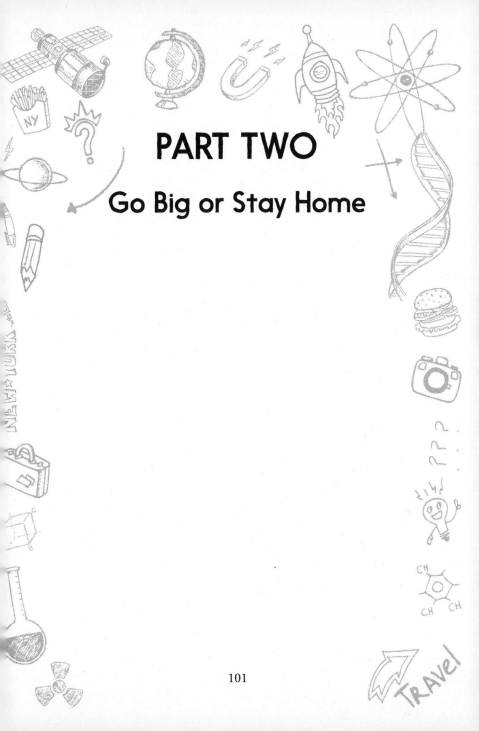

20

Max and Alexei left the small conference room and headed up the hall to the larger one where the entire team was assembled.

"Oh, good," said Ben when they entered. "Everybody? This is Hana's replacement, Alexei."

"Dude's a botanist?" cracked Keeto. "Because my mom's lawn needs mowing…"

"He's a humanist," said Max.

"Um, we're all humans," said Klaus. "Not much of a specialty, bro."

"Humanists," explained Alexei, with his winning smile,

"study the humanities. You know, languages, literature, philosophy, history..."

Klaus flapped a hand at Alexei. "You mean all the useless stuff they made me study in university?"

Alexei's smiled brightened. Max could tell the guy didn't take himself too seriously (unlike, say, Klaus).

"Yeah," said Alexei. "That's basically correct. I majored in all the subjects you guys had to suffer through before they'd let you go to your science classes and play around with really cool lab equipment."

Now the whole group laughed. Alexei was super charming.

Siobhan caught Max's eye and winked. Could she tell that Max was, maybe, possibly, crushing on the new kid? She'd had a similar crush on Ben but, lately, Ben had been kind of aloof and distant. He hadn't confided in Max in months, it seemed. Alexei, on the other hand, was a breath of fresh air. Maybe because he wasn't all about the science.

"Welcome, Alexei," said Anna. "Ben brought me on board to sharpen the CMI's messaging. Working together, I think we can really shape and contextualize our narrative going forward."

Alexei nodded. "Sure. Or we could just, you know, tell good stories."

"That, too," said Anna, smiling.

"There's, uh, someone else I'd like you guys to meet," said Ben. He punched some buttons on a control console to open a video chat. The face of a man in a business suit appeared on a large monitor.

Max wasn't really looking at the man. She was focused on the shimmering silver logo mounted on the wall behind him: BPW Petroleum.

"Guys," said Ben, "meet our new corporate sponsor, all the way from Australia, Mr. Oliver Woodside. He's an executive at one of Australia's, uh, largest oil and gas companies."

"G'day, mates," said the smiling middle-aged man on the video screen.

There was silence around the conference table.

Ben fidgeted nervously at the collar of his black T-shirt. "Uh, Mr. Woodside and BPW have matched all the money I've put up for our next big project, which, um, was a lot of money."

"Happy to lend a hand," said Mr. Woodside, cheerfully.

The entire CMI team was still gawking at the video

screen in disbelief. *An oil company was going to help them fight global warming?* Impossible.

Finally, Siobhan raised her hand.

"Yes, Siobhan?" said Ben.

"He's a bloomin' oil company executive? What the blazes are you thinkin', Ben?"

Mr. Woodside's cheery smile drooped a little.

Siobhan kept going. "They're the ones who profit from fossil fuel and carbon emissions. They're the oil-sucking vampires who, for decades, have misled the public and helped spread climate change denial."

"Oh," scoffed Klaus. "You mean they're the ones who helped spread the truth against a tsunami of fake science?" Klaus gave the oil man a double thumbs-up. "The ones who've kept our cars running and our homes heated? Good to have you on board, Mr. Woodside."

"Thank you, young man," said the oil executive.

"Mr. Abercrombie?" said Annika, her German accent more clipped than usual. "It is not even remotely logical that an oil executive, or his company, should be involved in our current climate crisis efforts."

"Why did you even seek out a corporate sponsor?" asked Vihaan. "It's not like we're NASCAR drivers..."

"Yeah," said Toma. "You're rich enough to sponsor everything yourself, right? What's up with this whole 'matching funds' situation?"

Ben blinked repeatedly before answering. "I, uh, in this particular instance, because of the scope of the project, not to mention my investments in some other areas, needed the help." He sounded like he was hiding something.

Is he having some kind of serious financial trouble? Max wondered. *Is that why Ben seemed so distant and preoccupied? Is that why Charl and Isabl aren't traveling with the team anymore? Maybe Ben can't afford to pay their salaries. Did he, somehow, blow his inherited fortune?*

"You guys?" Alexei said to the group grumbling around the table. "Maybe we should hear what Mr. Woodside and Ben are planning for the CMI." He turned to Anna, the marketing maven, and smiled. "Right, Anna? BPW's sponsorship might help us widen our communication platform."

"Exactly!" said Anna, picking up on Alexei's train of thought. "If we're going to tell a story about how we're all in this together, who better to add to the story line than a big oil company?" She turned to the video monitor. "Mr. Woodside? Do you have children?"

The man nodded. "Three. All of them a little younger than you lot."

"And you want them to live a long and healthy life, correct?"

"I surely do."

"BOOM!" said Anna. "We have our story."

Alexei grinned and shot Max a wink. "We surely do. Because, like Anna said, we're all in this together."

21

"Okay," said Ben. "Thanks, Alexei and Anna, for helping, you know, frame this for the, uh, group. There's another reason why I decided we should team up with BPW Petroleum. They're already working on something big that we can, you know, piggyback on. It's a way to fight global warming using geoengineering."

"Then I'm all ears," said Siobhan, the geoscientist.

Klaus looked ready to make a joke about Siobhan's ears until she glared at him hard—as if she knew what he was thinking. So Klaus turned his attention to the video screen.

"Great, Mr. Woodside," he said. "Let's use geoengineering to fight something that you and I both know doesn't really exist. Or we could just waste time watching paint dry."

"Mr. Woodside?" said Max, taking charge of the conference room because, well, somebody had to. Ben wasn't keen on conflict. It's why he usually didn't join the group in the field. "What's your big idea?"

"Something we've already started tinkering with down here in Oz," said the businessman. "Marine cloud brightening."

"A promisin' option," said Siobhan, softening slightly.

"How do you brighten clouds?" asked Keeto. "Shine spotlights on the puffy ones that look like horsies and duckies?"

Klaus slapped Keeto a high five. They were such boys.

"Actually," said Siobhan, "it's one of the most talked-about theoretical geoengineerin' options for coolin' down the planet."

"That's right," said Mr. Woodside. "BPW gave a very generous research grant to a local university to kick-start their work on the project. Now, with young Benjamin's help, and your involvement, we're ready to show the world what we've been up to. It involves spraying salt water from ships up into the clouds."

Siobhan nodded and took over explaining "cloud brightening" to her teammates.

"The salt facilitates the condensation of water vapor into liquid, generating water droplets. The more water droplets that are created, the larger and *brighter* the clouds will appear. These brighter clouds will reflect more sunlight and help cool the planet."

"So it's like giving the earth a pair of sunglasses," observed Alexei. "Mirrored sunglasses."

"Exactly," said Siobhan.

"I loved this idea the instant I heard about it," said Ben. "It's big. It's bold."

"It'll definitely grab people's attention," added Anna.

Now Max raised her hand.

"Yes, Max?" said Ben.

"If the project is already underway..."

"Oh, it is," said Mr. Woodside. "With Benjamin's help, we've put together enough financing to equip a fleet of boats with all the pumps and nozzles and gear they need to give a good spritzing to the clouds hovering over the Great Barrier Reef."

"So why do you need us?" asked Max.

"Because," said Anna, as if the answer were obvious,

"you just addressed the United Nations, Max. The world is looking to you, the new Einstein, for your genius leadership on dealing with the climate crisis. If you're on one of those cloud-brightening boats, I guarantee all the majors will cover the story. Siobhan should be there, too. To talk about the geoscience behind the cloud brightening. With the CMI on the scene, the press will turn what used to be a college research project into the top story of the news cycle."

"Especially after we blow it up big," said Ben, sounding way more excited than he usually did. "BPW and I bought a whole fleet of ships. Lots and lots of boats."

"It'll give us great optics," said Anna.

"And an excellent, hopeful story," said Alexei. "Everyone loves a good redemption tale. With the help of Max Einstein and the Change Makers Institute, Mr. Woodside and BPW will be like Ebenezer Scrooge waking up on Christmas morning, giddy about changing their wicked ways and doing good in the world while they still have time."

Everybody in the room was staring at Alexei. Even Mr. Woodside on the video monitor.

"Crikey," said Mr. Woodside. "You're good, young man."

"Because," said Ben, "he knows how to tell a good story."

"And," added Max, "he can do it in all sorts of different languages."

"Max?" said Ben. "You, Siobhan, Alexei, and Anna should pack your bags. You four leave for Australia tomorrow on my solar-powered jet. The rest of the team will remain here in New York City with me. We'll brainstorm more big and bold global warming solutions. I've arranged dorms and study space for you all at Max's alma mater, NYU."

"Can Klaus come with us to Australia?" Max asked.

Ben looked puzzled. He was probably wondering why Max wanted a global warming skeptic on a mission to fight global warming.

"We should also bring Leo," said Max. "Just in case we encounter some unforeseen complications or computations."

"And where Leo goes," said Klaus, "it's usually good if I tag along, too."

Ben considered Max's suggestion, then nodded. "Fine. Klaus? Prep Leo and be ready to leave first thing tomorrow."

"No problem." He turned to the video monitor. "Mr. Woodside? How are the sausages down under?"

"You mean our snags and bangers?" said the oil exec with a laugh. "The best in the world."

"Great," said Klaus. "So now I actually have a real reason for visiting Australia."

Max shook her head and grinned. She was glad Klaus was coming with them. Because if she could convince him that global warming was a real threat, she could probably convince anybody.

22

"I wish we could go to Australia and stay in New York at the same time," Alexei said to Max as they ate lunch together in a small salad place.

It reminded Max of the meals she used to have with Ben. There were more butterflies in her stomach than food.

"But," Alexei continued, "as excited as I am about the cloud-brightening idea and flying to Australia, I'm not sure 'big and bold' is the only way to go. Sometimes, the big solution is lots of little solutions."

"Well," said Max, veering off into her comfort zone (all things Albert Einstein), "with what we call 'quantum

superposition,' it *is* possible for giant molecules of matter to occupy two different places at once."

"Seriously?"

Max nodded. "Because every particle is also a wave..."

"So we could be in New York and Australia at the same time?"

"Theoretically. Of course, Professor Einstein didn't really like the theory. He dismissed quantum entanglement—the ability of separated objects to share a condition or state—as 'spooky action at a distance.'"

Alexei had a blank look on his face.

"Sorry," said Max. "TMS. Too much science."

"That's okay. I like your science. I just wanted to check out some of the other, smaller, global warming solutions being tried right here in New York City. Sure, the cloud-brightening show with all the boats spraying salt water up into the sky will be spectacular and tell an amazing story. But there are so many simpler solutions. They make good stories, too...if not good TV. There's one in particular that I'd love to see."

"So, let's go check it out. We have time. We're not hopping on the solar jet until first thing tomorrow morning."

"Good idea. Oh, and guess what?"

"What?"

"This simple solution I want to check out? It involves botany!"

Alexei and Max hailed a taxi and headed across town.

"Guess we should've told Ben or Anna where we're going," said Max as the cab rumbled along 34th Street.

"Nah. Anna would've alerted the media. This will be better if we fly under the radar. You'll get to take it all in without worrying about all the cameras watching you take it in."

Alexei wanted to quietly visit the Jacob K. Javits Convention Center in Midtown Manhattan.

"It has the second-largest green roof in America," Alexei explained. "They took a heat-absorbing, old-fashioned, black tar roof and turned it into seven acres of green meadows. It's bigger than five football fields. It's botany!"

"Cool," said Max.

"Exactly," said Alexei, thumbing his phone to call up some stats. "In fact, with grass and dirt and layers of waterproofing fabric, the green roof gives them great insulation. It's reduced the convention center's overall cooling and heating costs by twenty-five percent. It also prevents six point eight million gallons of rainwater runoff from polluting the nearby Hudson River every year."

Max and Alexei climbed out of their cab and approached the gigantic glass cube building on foot. While they walked, Alexei told Max more stuff he'd googled, like how the green roof not only helped New York City slash carbon emissions—it had also become something of a bird, bat, and bee sanctuary.

"They have their own beehives up there and harvest the honey," Alexei explained.

There were no conventions scheduled at the Javits Center that day, so the cavernous place was mostly deserted. Max and Alexei found a uniformed security guard who recognized Max from all the coverage of her UN speech. He showed her and Alexei how to go up to the roof.

"We're officially closed for tours up there today," he said, "but you two can go for a quick look."

"Thank you," said Max.

"You kids are gonna love it. I like to eat my lunch up there sometimes. Very peaceful, know what I mean? Just take that elevator to the top floor and then use the staircase. The doors to the roof are unlocked."

"Thanks," said Max.

After giving the guard an autograph, she and Alexei rode the elevator to the top floor and found the doorway to the staircase leading to the roof. They bounded up the stairs to a set of double doors with handles. While Alexei pushed them open, Max noticed a bright-red fire hose cabinet mounted on the wall beside the door.

Later, she'd be glad she did.

23

"Whoa . . ."

Max and Alexei were in awe as they stepped out onto the roof.

"This is so cool," said Max.

"Fantastic," Alexei agreed.

The whole area in front of them was a vast sea of green.

"It's like we landed in a meadow in the middle of Kansas," said Max.

Alexei laughed. "Except we're in the middle of Manhattan."

Bees were buzzing in and out of their wooden hives. Birds were swooping down for gentle landings on the grass.

"I think that's a herring seagull," said Alexei, pointing

to a white bird taking flight from its perch in the rooftop meadow.

Max looked to where he was pointing.

And didn't like what she saw.

Because a sleek black helicopter had just darted up from the nearby river. It banked left and swooped down to hover over the roof. Someone on board tossed out a rope ladder. It unspooled itself all the way down to a patch of grass at the far edge of the field.

Two commandos, dressed in black fatigues, scurried out of the chopper's side door and clambered down the ladder.

And both of them were carrying weapons.

"We need to leave," Max shouted at Alexei. "Now!"

The two armed mercenaries were nearing the bottom rung of the rope ladder.

"Who are those guys?" Alexei shouted back.

"I don't know!" said Max, even though she suspected the men in black fatigues were related to the men in white camo who had chased her and Siobhan across the glacier in Greenland. "But I don't think they're convention center security guards."

Max and Alexei raced for the doors. Far behind them,

they could hear the thud of boots touching down on the garden's concrete pavers.

Now Max heard a voice shouting, *"Tam! Eta dver'! Bystro!"*

She looked to Alexei. He nodded. He recognized the language.

"Russian," he said, yanking open the double doors.

Max and Alexei leaped inside and let the metal doors slam shut behind them.

Suddenly, there was a soft *THWICK!* followed by a circle of streaming sunlight.

"Their weapons have sound suppressors on the muzzles," said Max, quickly. "They reduce the acoustic intensity of the gunshot by modulating the speed and pressure of its propellant gas."

"This is no time for a physics lesson, Max!" Alexei ducked down and grabbed both handles of the double doors. "I don't know how to lock these doors! We don't have a key!"

Alexei was panicking. Max couldn't blame the guy. He wasn't used to being shot at. Max? Beginning on that glacier, it seemed to be becoming a routine thing.

THWICK! Another bullet sliced through the door. This time on the right.

"Stand back," Max ordered Alexei.

"But...the doors...they're not locked..."

"They will be." Max sprang into action. "Call nine-one-one."

Alexei leaned up against the cinder-block wall and made the call.

Max tugged open the glass door to the bright-red fire-hose cabinet and pulled out several yards of heavy line. Crouching and pulling the fire hose behind her, she moved to the double doors—making certain to stay low, beneath the mysterious pursuers' targeting zone, which seemed to be about four feet above the floor.

Because they're going for a head or chest shot, Max figured.

They meant business.

SWICK. Another bullet burst through the top of the door, trailed by a stream of sunlight.

There was the thumping roar of a helicopter powering up and flying away.

The two gunmen were on their own. Their ride had left the scene. Max figured the bad guys' chopper *had* to take off. The NYPD had helicopters, too.

Max nimbly fed the nozzle of the fire hose through one door handle and then the other. She threaded enough of the canvas line through the door handles so she could double back and loop the nozzle around its hose like she was knotting off a bulky shoelace.

"The police are on their way," Alexei shouted.

"Great. Help me tighten this."

Alexei put away his phone and helped Max pull down on the pointed nozzle until the hose cinched on itself.

"You think that will hold them?" asked Alexei when the line was secured on itself.

"Maybe," said Max. "But we can make the seal even tighter."

"How?"

"More physics."

She raced back to the fire hose cabinet and twisted open its valve. Water gushed into the hose. In a flash, the flat canvas ribbon inflated like a python that'd just swallowed too many watermelons.

The hose looped through the door handles bulged. The doors creaked as the swollen hose tightened and secured its grip.

"The hydraulic pressure inside a fire hose typically ranges from three hundred to twelve hundred pounds per square inch," Max explained.

"So it can keep those doors closed better than any lock!" said Alexei.

"Exactly."

Suddenly, the doors jerked. Someone outside was yanking on them. Hard. The doors shook but they didn't budge. The water pressure had a very firm grip on the handles. Outside, fists started banging on the doors. In the distance, Max heard sirens. Lots of them.

"*Nam nuzhno ubirat'sya otsyuda! Seychas!*" shouted one of their attackers on the other side of the door.

Max looked to Alexei.

He was breathing a little less rapidly. He was even smiling again. Slightly.

"They're leaving," he translated, with a sigh. "Now."

24

"We don't know who they were or where they went," Max told Ben. "We heard their helicopter take off, but we don't know what happened to the two goons with the guns who chased us across the roof. They were gone by the time the NYPD swarmed the rooftop garden."

"I bet they rappelled down the back wall or used zip lines," said Alexei. "The river is right there. They might've had a getaway boat stashed along the piers in the Hudson. Maybe scuba gear..."

Ben sighed. "I'm so, so sorry about this, Max."

"Hey, Alexei had to dodge a few bullets, too," Max reminded him.

"I know," said Ben. He turned to Alexei and gave a goofy grin. "Welcome to the team, Alexei."

Ben was trying to make a joke. Alexei's lips crinkled up into a smile. Max's didn't. The three of them were sitting around a table in the living room of Ben's hotel suite.

"We need Charl and Isabl," Max said to Ben, angrily. "You don't have to be a genius to realize someone new is out to stop us. This incident up on the roof at the Javits Center can't be separated from the attack on the glacier."

Alexei turned to her. "You were attacked on a glacier?"

Max nodded. "There was a sleek black helicopter involved in that little incident, too. If the Corp is really gone, Ben, then somebody new is out to get us."

"Actually," said Ben, who sometimes said things out loud that he probably shouldn't, "I think someone new is out to get *you,* Max."

"Gee, thanks, Ben. You know how to make a kid feel safe. Oh, for what it's worth, today's team was speaking Russian."

She checked Alexei's handsome Russian face for the slightest tell. There wasn't one. If he was a spy, he was a good one.

Ben nodded thoughtfully. "The oil oligarchs in Russia,

I'm sure, don't like us joining the crusade against global warming. In fact, they were all very happy when Russia's arctic permafrost started melting. It opened up a lot of new land for them to drill for oil and gas..."

"Whoever's after us—or after *me*—they have weapons," said Max. "We need Charl and Isabl, Ben. We shouldn't go to Australia without them."

"Agreed," said Ben. "I'll, you know, make the arrangements. Have them meet you when you land in Australia. You'll just have to be extra careful when you get off the plane in Hawaii."

Alexei arched an eyebrow. "Hawaii? I'm confused. I thought we were flying to Australia."

"Layover," said Max, who'd already done the mileage math in her head. "The solar-powered plane will need to recharge its batteries, right, Ben?"

Ben nodded. Reluctantly.

Max kept going. "No way will we have enough power to fly the ten thousand miles from New York City to Australia on one charge."

Ben sighed. "You'll have to take a quick break in Honolulu and let the jet sunbathe for a little while. Now, in the future, when everybody is flying solar-powered planes, we could just swap out batteries in Hawaii; no sunbathing required."

"Too bad we can't just fast-forward into the future," said Alexei.

"Yeah," said Ben. "That'd be great."

Then they both laughed. Once again, Max did not.

She was too busy wishing she could rewind into the past. She'd love to live in whatever year it would have to be for people not to be chasing after her with guns equipped with suppressors.

Max was still pondering time travel that night while she packed her bags for the trip to Australia and the cloud-brightening demonstration over the Great Barrier Reef.

A thought popped into her head, so she grabbed her journal and started doodling.

Could she somehow re-create what her parents had done in their basement laboratory but reverse the outcome?

Could she use Einstein's theory of relativity and find a way to travel *backward* in time?

Or maybe she would have to come up with a new theory. After all, the world had learned an awful lot since 1955 when Albert Einstein passed away.

Could Max rejoin her family, the parents she only

remembered as faint shapes and shadows, and, this time, crawl away from the future instead of into it?

Maybe time could be manipulated the same way atoms could. Her head was full of quantum theories and "arrow of time" imagery when she felt as if someone was looking over her shoulder, studying the doodles fueling her drifting thought experiment.

She slowly turned around in her chair.

And saw him.

Albert Einstein.

The real deal.

The one who had flickered in and out of view outside the noodle shop.

"Hello, Dorothy," he said again, his voice breaking up as if it was on a weak radio station you can't quite tune in to as you whiz down the highway. "United...Nations... save the world...grave danger..."

And then, he was gone.

25

The next morning, Max, Alexei, Anna, Siobhan, Klaus, and Leo took off for Australia on Ben's prototype solar-powered jet.

This time, Leo, the robot, was up front with the pilots, helping them fly the aircraft. The automaton was great for autopiloting a plane.

"This is amazing," said Alexei as the craft silently drifted across the United States at an altitude of thirty thousand feet.

"It's all right," said Siobhan, trying her best to sound nonchalant. "But this is my second jaunt on the jet."

"Mine, too," said Max, playfully slugging Siobhan in the shoulder. "And it's still absolutely amazing."

"I know," said Siobhan, losing all her cool composure. "Bloomin' fantastic!"

"I've already fed this out to some friendly reporters," said Anna. She slid her hand across the empty air as if she were reading a news ticker. "'Max Einstein Flies Off to Execute Global Warming Solution in a Global Warming Solution: The World's First Solar-Powered Jet Aircraft.'"

"Let's just hope we don't drop like a rock when we pass through some clouds," said Klaus, his arms folded across his chest.

"Batteries!" shouted Max, Siobhan, Alexei, and Anna, as if they were reminding Klaus for the ten millionth time.

"They're quite good for storing electricity, Klaus," said Siobhan. "You should try them. Oh, wait. You already have. In your phone. Maybe you just need some fresh ones for your brain."

"This whole mission is such a complete waste of our time," Klaus huffed. "We're not doing real science. We're not even part of the solution. It's just a publicity stunt. Some PR spin for an Australian oil company." He turned to Alexei with a smirk on his face. "Shouldn't they be the villains in this story, Mr. I-Studied-the-Humanities?"

Alexei grinned. "Only in the cliché version of the tale. In ours, they're fellow humans working toward an answer and a brighter future."

"Exactly," said Anna. "We're spotlighting this joint effort with BPW because we need to call attention to global warming and also offer up some possible solutions. The fact that even big oil recognizes the problem is huge for us."

"Global warming," said Klaus dismissively. "It's a hoax made up by environmental extremists, the fake news media, and liberals looking for an excuse for more big government or, worse, a world government run by Max's pals back at the UN. That's why they were all standing up and cheering for your speech, by the way."

"Here you go," said Siobhan, handing Klaus a laminated card listing more than three dozen organizations such as NASA, NOAA, and others from all around the globe. "Every major scientific institution in the world with a mandate to deal with climate, ocean, and/or atmosphere agrees with geoscientists like me that the earth's climate is warming rapidly and the number one cause is human carbon dioxide emissions."

"More fake news," said Klaus. "You said it yourself. They're *world* organizations so of course they're promoting the one-world government propaganda coming out of the UN."

Siobhan was about to say something when Leo's voice came over the public address system in the jet's cabin.

"This is not the captain speaking. However, she has advised me that we are beginning our initial descent into Honolulu and should be on the ground in Hawaii shortly. Kindly fasten your seat belts."

"Oh," chuckled Klaus. "And why are we landing? Because Ben's solar jet needs to lay out in the sun and recharge its batteries."

"So?" said Anna. "A petroleum-powered plane couldn't fly nonstop from New York to Australia without refueling, either."

"Qantas, the Australian airline, is working on it," countered Klaus. "Plus, it only takes a few minutes to pump gas into a plane's wings. How long does this bird have to sit on the runway and soak up the sunshine?"

The argument continued all the way down to the Honolulu airport.

Unfortunately, it was raining when the CMI team

landed. The sun was hidden behind a tower of billowy black clouds.

Klaus smirked.

"Guess it's going to take even longer to recharge our batteries, huh, guys?"

26

Finally, the sun came out.

"It'll be about six more hours before we're ready to take off again," reported the solar jet's pilot.

"Even though the companies working with Benjamin have made astronomical strides in battery density," said Leo, "they are extremely expensive so, currently, there are no spares."

"So what do we do while the plane suns itself?" asked Klaus.

"We're going to go play golf," said the pilot, gesturing to her copilot.

Max was torn.

On the one hand, she didn't want to bump into any more Russian thugs who might've followed her and the solar-powered jet to Hawaii (especially since Anna had already alerted the media about the CMI's plans).

On the other hand, they'd already been sitting around for nearly three hours waiting for the sun to break through the clouds. She couldn't take six more hours of basically doing nothing. Max bored easily. She preferred being a body in motion that stayed in motion.

She did a quick risk/reward analysis while Klaus chomped a big bite out of a very garlicky sausage he'd just found buried in his backpack. When he belched, the air smelled even worse.

That sealed the deal.

"We should head out and explore the island," said Max. "After all, climate change will really affect Hawaii and all the other islands in the world. I could also use some, uh, fresh air."

She fanned the stink cloud hovering in front of her face.

"Good idea," said Alexei, and Max noticed his slight accent again.

His slight Russian accent.

"Too right," said Siobhan. "Rising sea levels—of maybe even eight to ten feet—are Hawaii's and every other island's worse nightmare. And then there are all the rare birds here that could go extinct thanks to disease-carrying mosquitoes invading their mountain habitats due to warmer weather."

Klaus chomped another bite out of his sausage, shook his head, and rolled his eyes. "It's a ho-oax," he singsonged. "A ho-oooax!"

"I can arrange ground transportation for you," offered Leo. "Perhaps motorized golf carts?"

"Great idea," said Anna, holding up her phone. "I'll grab some action shots of you guys studying the damage already being done here."

"And," said Alexei, "let's hope we can also find some stories of what these Pacific islands are doing to combat climate change."

"They don't need to do anything!" blurted Klaus. "These islands have taken care of themselves for centuries."

"Oh, yeah?" said Siobhan. "Tell it to the banana trees."

"What?"

She turned to Leo. "Organize those golf carts, mate."

"And make sure they're electric!" said Anna.

"Uh, no thank you," said Klaus. "I want one that runs on gasoline."

"You mean a utility vehicle," said Leo.

"Call it what you want. I just don't want the batteries conking out on me like they did on Ben's toy jet."

About an hour later, the two carts were parked at a banana plantation near Oʻahu, twelve miles north of the Honolulu airport.

Leo had driven Klaus in the gas-powered vehicle. Max piloted the electric cart with Anna, Siobhan, and Alexei as passengers. Leo and Klaus arrived first. In fact, they'd beaten Max and her puttering electric cart by fifteen minutes.

Max didn't care. She was just glad their little caravan hadn't been attacked by an angry Russian oligarch's commando hit squad. She so wished Charl and Isabl had met the jet in Hawaii.

"This is where we could really use Hana," said Siobhan, leading the others into a stand of banana trees.

"Excuse me?" said Max, who, maybe more than anybody, remembered Hana's stinging betrayal of the team on their last mission.

"A botanist," Siobhan explained. "As you guys could probably guess, Hawaii is the only significant commercial producer of bananas in the United States because it's the only state with the right tropical climate." She held up an elephant-ear-sized leaf on a nearby banana tree. Its green was streaked with black. "This is a fungus known as black sigatoka," she explained. "It can reduce fruit production on infected plants by up to eighty percent."

"And what does this have to do with the whole global warming con job?" asked Klaus.

"The fungus thrives on wet leaves," Siobhan explained, doing her best not to erupt like a Hawaiian volcano and bite off Klaus's head. "Climate change has increased the amount of rainfall here in Hawaii and elsewhere in the banana-producing world."

"Whoa," said Klaus. "I thought you guys said global warming brings on droughts?"

"It does," said Max.

"Really?" said Klaus. "Then why is Siobhan talking about heavy rainfall, which, hello, is the exact opposite of a drought?"

"Climate warming," Max tried to explain, "increases evaporation on land. That leads to drought and wildfires.

Meanwhile, all that moisture sucked out of the land leads to bigger, heavier, more extreme rain and snowstorms elsewhere."

"Snow?" said Klaus. "How can it snow at all if the whole planet is warming?"

Siobhan had finally heard enough from Klaus.

"Ah, put a sock in it, Klaus."

Max had had enough of Klaus, too. But she had a better idea than stuffing a sock in his mouth.

When Klaus and Leo weren't looking, Max grabbed a banana off a tree and jammed it up the tailpipe of Klaus's gas-powered cart.

"Um, Max?" asked Alexei, who'd seen her insert the fruit, "what are you doing?"

"Simple science," Max replied with a wink. "Internal combustion engines operating on fossil fuels have to breathe in order to burn gas. They have to inhale oxygen through their intake manifolds and exhale carbon dioxide through the tailpipe. You block either end, you might as well be sitting in a solar-powered electric jet with a dead battery."

And that's why Max and her crew made it back to the

Honolulu airport long before Klaus and Leo even figured out what was wrong with their gas-powered vehicle.

When they were safely back in the air, Klaus pouted the whole way to Australia.

Which was fine by Max.

When Klaus pouted, he didn't talk so much.

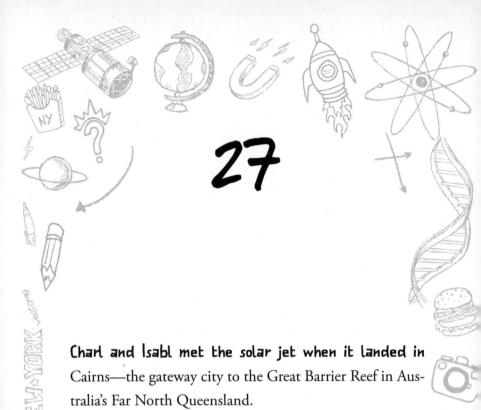

27

Charl and Isabl met the solar jet when it landed in Cairns—the gateway city to the Great Barrier Reef in Australia's Far North Queensland.

Max could've hugged them. Except she knew they weren't huggers.

As usual, the duo were decked out in what Max thought of as safari clothes. Lots of khaki. Lots of pockets. Lots of places to hide stuff.

Neither Charl nor Isabl had a last name that they cared to share with anyone, but they were both very skilled in the use of tactical weapons. Isabl also had mad skills behind the wheel of any vehicle. She could've starred in one of

those *Fast and Furious* movies—if they were even faster and a little more furious.

Together, Charl and Isabl were like a two-person SWAT team. Their goal? Protect Max and the CMI team at all costs. Max was relieved that Ben had agreed to hire them again. But she had to wonder: *Had the solar-powered jet with its "extremely expensive" batteries put a major dent in the benefactor's bank account? And what about the "fleet of boats" for the cloud-brightening demonstration? How expensive was that?*

Max actually knew the answer to that last question: Expensive enough that Ben had to go searching for a corporate sponsor to share the costs of the Australian Cloud-Brightening Brigade (Alexei had come up with that name).

"Ben?" Charl said into his secure satellite phone. Both he and Isabl had hard-to-place accents. Eastern Europe? The Middle East? "The team has safely arrived in Cairns."

Ben was still in New York, remotely monitoring the Australian project, with the rest of the CMI geniuses. *Another sign of financial strain?* In the past, the whole CMI team went everywhere together, no matter the cost.

"Roger that," Charl said to Ben, and then he closed up the phone. "We need to head up to the port," he told the group. "The fleet awaits."

"Into the van, everybody," said Isabl.

"Hey, Isabl?" said Klaus as the team climbed into the hulky black vehicle. "You better check your tailpipe."

"What for?"

"Bananas," offered Leo. "They can prove to be quite a hindrance to gas-powered internal combustion engines."

Isabl patted the side of their ride. "Good thing this is a hybrid."

BPW Petroleum and Ben had organized a fleet of six dozen flat barges at Port Douglas, about an hour north of Cairns. Seventy-two vessels. It was a very impressive armada.

When Max and her team arrived on the scene, it was obvious that Anna had done her advance work. The docks were swarming with television camera crews and reporters.

And they all wanted to talk to Max. Actually, they all wanted to scream questions at her.

"What brings you down under, Max?" hollered an Australian reporter.

Anna leaned in to answer for her: "A solar-powered jet!"

Max took over from there. "We're here to draw attention to some of the big, bold ideas scientists all over the world are coming up with to battle climate change."

"That's right," said Mr. Woodside, the oil company executive, sidling up to Max so he could poke his head into camera range. "At BPW, we say a brighter tomorrow begins today. That's why we at BPW are proud sponsors of this cloud-brightening project."

Okay, Max thought. *He mentioned his company's name. Twice. Guess he got what he paid for.*

"Max Einstein will speak and gladly answer all your questions immediately after the demonstration," Anna told the press. "Right now, the Changer Makers Institute needs to head down to the boats and start brightening the sky along with our friends and colleagues from the university and, of course, BPW, where, as you heard, a brighter tomorrow begins today."

Okay. Make that three plugs for Ben's corporate partner.

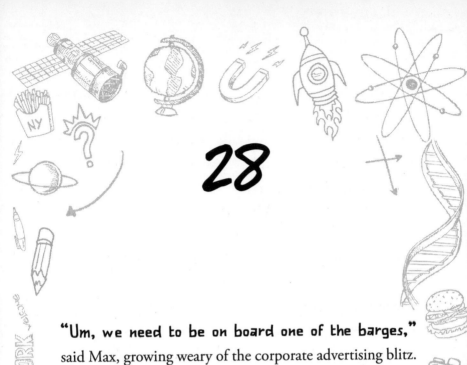

28

"**Um, we need to be on board one of the barges,**" said Max, growing weary of the corporate advertising blitz. "Guys? Follow me."

She led the way down to the dock. Alexei, Klaus, Siobhan, and Leo were right behind her. Charl and Isabl flanked the CMI kids, scanning the crowd, looking for any potential trouble. Anna and Mr. Woodside brought up the rear so they could keep working the press mob trailing behind Max and the team.

There were seventy-two flatboats lined up in the harbor. All of them bright white and flying BPW Petroleum banners.

"What are those big things in their sterns?" asked a reporter from CNN. "They look like jet engines."

Anna turned to the team's trusty robot. "Leo? Can you download the deets?"

"Of course." The automaton with the face of a choirboy turned to the cluster of cameras and microphones. They all pushed in for a close-up. Super smart, chattering robots made good TV. "Those are modified turbines, each equipped with one hundred high-pressure nozzles that will spray trillions of nano-sized ocean salt crystals up into the air. As the water droplets evaporate, bright salt crystals will remain to reflect away incoming solar radiation."

"Think of it as a giant pair of mirrored sunglasses for the coral reef," offered Alexei, repeating his easy-to-understand analogy. The press corps looked like they loved that simple way to explain the science to their audiences. Several reporters scribbled Alexei's words on their notepads.

"That's right," said Leo. "Scaled up, this marine cloud–brightening technique could shade and cool the Great Barrier Reef, protecting its coral from the dangerous bleaching caused by rising global temperatures."

"We could also build spray towers on land," said Siobhan, "all along the shoreline. We could float them on barges."

"Like brave firefighters everywhere," said Alexei, "we

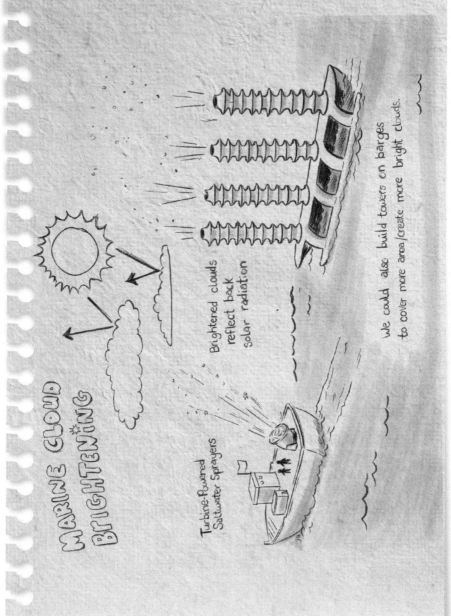

can spray the ocean's salt water to help cool down and, eventually, extinguish global warming."

More reporters scribbled more notes. Max grinned. Alexei definitely had an interesting way of translating science into a story.

"We're, uh, excited to show you how science can help save the planet," said Max, who still wished somebody else had been chosen to be the master of ceremonies for this event. "Please follow along behind us in your own boats."

The press climbed aboard several follow craft as Max and her team boarded their vessel, which had one of the angled turbine engines aiming up at the sky.

Klaus, who hadn't said anything since the event began, edged his way over to where Max stood on the deck. He tapped the huge turbine.

"This baby run on jet fuel?" he asked.

"Yeah," said Max.

"Thought so," smirked Klaus.

Max understood his unspoken meaning. They were about to generate carbon emissions to fight the effects of carbon emissions.

"Good luck, Max," said Klaus, a little snidely. "You're going to need it."

29

The fleet of seventy-two barges swept out into the Coral Sea.

A half dozen media boats trailed behind the CMI vessel as it bounded across the choppy water. Charl and Isabl, their eyes shaded by mirrored sunglasses, were on full alert, scanning the horizon and the cloudy sky for any incoming threats.

Klaus had goosed Leo's voice amplification system so he could address the media in the boats trailing the barges.

"I set Leo's volume at eleven," he joked. "And, if you also want to say stuff, use this." He handed Max a wireless microphone. "It's Bluetoothed into Leo's public address system."

Max reluctantly took the microphone. "I think I'll let Leo handle most of the talking."

"Bad idea," said Anna. "You're the one everybody wants to hear from, Max, not the Tin Man."

"Watch it," snapped Klaus, only half-kidding. "That's my boy-bot you're talking about."

"Let Leo handle the setup," said Max. "Siobhan and I will talk about some of the science once we start the demonstration."

"Better you two than me," joked Alexei.

Leo moved to the stern of the barge and showed the cameras in the media boats a small, data-gathering drone. "Ladies and gentlemen, once we commence spraying salt water into the clouds, I will be sending up and operating a squadron of remote-controlled drones."

"Why?" shouted the nearest reporter.

"The drones will help us map out how the plume we're creating is blending into the clouds and will measure the increased brightness."

Siobhan grabbed the microphone from Max. "As you

blokes probably know, the coral that makes up the Great Barrier Reef under all this water isn't a plant, even though it looks like one. Coral is a living creature, closely related to other sea creatures like sea anemones and jellyfish."

"Which everybody hates!" shouted Klaus, who loved being the class clown when he wasn't busy being the class climate-change-denier-in-chief.

Siobhan kept going. "When coral gets stressed by heat from rising sea temperatures, it expels the algae living in their tissues, turning the coral completely white. We call it coral bleaching, which can lead to coral death, which can upset the whole ecosystem down below. Coral reefs are home to twenty-five percent of the world's marine species. They're like an underwater version of the Amazon rain forest. If we don't reverse global warming, we're going to lose the reef and all the species that need it to survive."

"Or," shouted Klaus, "we can just feed the gnarly little boogers more algae."

Alexei looked to Max. Bringing Klaus on this "field trip" might've been a huge mistake. It was her turn to grab the microphone.

"Actually," she told the reporters, "what we're going to do is feed those clouds up there more water droplets in an attempt to make them brighter so they can reflect away more of the sun's rays and heat. Like Alexei said earlier, they'll be like mirrored sunglasses for the planet!"

Alexei gave her a "way to go" wink.

"And," said Anna, "the planet won't just look cool with those mirrored shades. It'll also BE cool!"

She earned a few chuckles.

"Leo?" said Max, as dramatically as she could. It was showtime! "Initiate the spraying."

Leo's robotic eyes blink-clicked six times in rapid succession. "Initiating."

"We're using our robotic friend's incredible AI as a command-and-control center to coordinate the actions of all the saltwater sprayers on all six dozen ships," Max explained. "They're like giant snow-making machines. We're taking seawater. Atomizing it. And spraying it out into the air with the hope that those droplets will rise, mix at the atmospheric boundary level, and, like I said, brighten the clouds a little bit. If we can do that, if we can reflect away some of the sunshine and cool down the ocean, it might stop some of that coral bleaching Siobhan was talking about."

The seventy-two boats started spraying a fine mist up into the air.

At first, it looked pretty impressive.

But, in a matter of minutes, it looked like what it was. Six dozen turbine-powered spray bottles spewing thin, wispy clouds of saltwater mist behind the barges.

It looked silly.

30

The gauzy clouds of airborne salt water quickly dissipated.

They were like a cluster of thin morning fog that burns away with the rising sun.

Max noticed that some of the reporters were shaking their heads in disbelief. A few were laughing. Several of the camera operators lowered their gear from their shoulders.

Spraying salt water up into the sky and watching it vanish didn't make for great television, no matter how many spray barges were in your fleet.

"This is bad," said Anna, looking slightly panicked. "These optics are horrible."

"The science is solid," said Max, feeling like somehow this humiliating debacle was all her fault, even though it hadn't even been her idea.

"The clouds are brightening," reported Leo, tracking data from the drones. "Sunshine is being reflected. The water will start to cool soon..."

But none of the media were impressed. One boat of reporters actually peeled off from the flotilla and headed back to shore.

Feeling queasy, Max looked over the port side railing and saw Mr. Oliver Woodside from BPW Petroleum with his team of PR people at the back of another barge spritzing salt water up into the air.

Mr. Woodside stood beneath a flapping BPW flag and raised a bullhorn.

"Ladies and gentlemen," he said, "as you may have gathered, even if we're successful out here, cloud brightening alone will not replace the need for reducing our carbon emissions. That's why we at BPW are at the forefront of developing cleaner fuels that produce fewer emissions when burned. We're doing everything we can to prevent the gasoline we *do* use—and will have to keep using for the foreseeable future to keep our economies humming—from getting any dirtier. Because a brighter tomorrow for all of us begins today."

"Crikey," Siobhan muttered. "We've been played. This whole thing was a publicity stunt for BPW Petroleum..."

All the cameras were trained on Mr. Woodside and the BPW Petroleum banner fluttering behind him. The media had lost all interest in Max, the CMI, and their chatty robot.

"I did not see this coming," muttered Anna. "This event is a total washout."

"Not exactly the whiz-bang ending we wanted for our story," added Alexei.

Klaus just smirked at Max. "Go big or stay home, huh? Guess we should've stayed home."

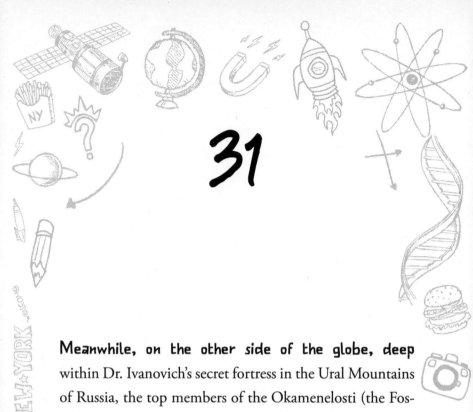

31

Meanwhile, on the other side of the globe, deep within Dr. Ivanovich's secret fortress in the Ural Mountains of Russia, the top members of the Okamenelosti (the Fossils) were celebrating the CMI's public humiliation.

The walls in the former castle's high-tech media room were lined with giant-screen TVs, all of them tuned to live satellite coverage from news networks that had been breathlessly focused on the "Australian Cloud-Brightening Brigade" and its young "world-changing" geniuses.

The assembled titans of the fossil fuel industry had been greatly enjoying the televised media accounts of Max Einstein and the Change Makers Institute's humiliating

cloud-spraying demonstration off the coast of Australia in the Coral Sea.

It looked ridiculous.

Seventy-two very expensive-looking, high-tech turbines spewing saltwater spray through hundreds of tiny nozzles up into the sky?

Hysterical.

"They look like such fools!" said an elegant woman with silver hair. "Little Max Einstein is an international joke. The UN must regret asking *her* to address their General Assembly."

Laughter echoed around the cavernous stone room.

Dr. Ivanovich raised his hand to silence the crowd.

"Ladies and gentlemen, you are correct. We are much closer to eliminating Max Einstein and her colleagues as a potential threat. In fact, I suspect it will be a long time before she, or any other young crusader, will be able to once again command the world's attention in regard to so-called climate change. Thanks to the massive coverage of this embarrassing experiment, we will soon be rid of *all* the youthful activists who have been clamoring for ill-advised action."

His audience applauded.

"Of course," Dr. Ivanovich continued, "there is still more work to be done. But that, my friends, is labor for another day. Today, we celebrate. Please. Enjoy the refreshments."

While his invited guests descended on the buffet tables, Dr. Ivanovich motioned for Vlad, his personal assistant, to come closer so they could speak in confidence.

"Send an encrypted text to Mr. Woodside in Australia," he whispered. "Thank him and BPW for their invaluable assistance in this cloud-brightening matter. Because of their involvement and financial investment, the whole world saw what a joke these young climate alarmists truly are. We will not forget BPW's efforts in our quest for the greater good, et cetera, et cetera. However, also remind Mr. Woodside that he needs to stop boasting about 'clean gasoline.' We have too much of the dirty variety left to sell."

The assistant nodded.

"Oh, and one more thing," Ivanovich said with a sly smile. "Contact our other assets in Australia. Instruct them to find out where Max Einstein will be traveling next. We must arrange to have someone on the ground there to greet her."

32

The press scrum at the docks was relentless.

"Seriously?" shouted one reporter. "Spraying water into the air is going to solve global warming and save the planet?"

Max hung her head. She *so* didn't want to be the "face" of this fiasco, which, really, wasn't a fiasco. Leo's tracking data from his squadron of hovering drones demonstrated that the clouds had indeed brightened. Somewhat. The water temperature had cooled. Slightly.

But "somewhat" and "slightly" never made for good television.

Klaus stepped forward and addressed the cameras. "We're also calling upon every kid in the world who happens

to have a squirt gun or Super Soaker or even a garden hose with a spray nozzle to join us and aim their water shooters straight up at the sky tomorrow at noon. That much spritzing ought to brighten even more clouds all over the globe!"

The reporters laughed and shook their heads in disbelief.

"Okay, Klaus," said Alexei out of the side of his mouth. "That's enough."

"Says who, Humanities Boy?"

"Ben," snapped Siobhan, waggling her phone in Klaus's face. "He just texted. Guess he was watching back in New York. He's calling off the mission."

Max sighed. "We should've called it off before we even started..."

"Let's load up the van," said Charl. He and Isabl looked a little on edge. They didn't like having the CMI team so exposed in front of the tight cluster of snickering press people. The mob of cameras and microphones would be great cover for any would-be bad actors and troublemakers.

"We need to head back to the airport," said Isabl.

"Not before I have a few words with Mr. Oliver Woodside," said Anna. She was seething. "He was so off-brand and off-strategy with that crack about clean gasoline."

She made a move to her right. Isabl restrained her with a quick grab of the elbow.

"It can wait," said Isabl. "We don't like the dynamics of this situation. Too many variables. We can't control the crowd. Klaus? Have Leo do that arm-swinging thing he does. Clear us a path to the vehicle."

"Do it, Klaus," barked Charl. "We need to be Oscar Mike—On the Move! Now."

Flustered, Klaus nervously tapped several spots on the glass face of Leo's control pad. The robot flailed his limbs and spoke in a repeating loop: "Stand aside, coming through! Stand aside, coming through!"

The terrified press people jumped out of the way. The CMI team made it to the van without incident.

And without answering any more questions.

Thirty minutes later, when the transport vehicle arrived at the airport and drove out to where Ben's solar jet was parked on the tarmac, Max noticed something peculiar.

The pilot and copilot were standing in front of the plane's nose with their rolling suitcases. They both had boarding passes in their hands.

You don't need a boarding pass when you are flying on a private solar-powered jet.

A luggage trolley attached to a ground services tug cart was parked near the jet's cargo hold. The bored man behind the wheel was idly thumbing his phone, waiting for...something.

"We all have to fly on commercial flights," the pilot announced when the CMI team climbed out of the van. "The Australian Civil Aviation Safety Authority has deemed our 'experimental aircraft' in violation of their certification requirements. They've impounded it. This solar jet isn't flying anywhere anytime soon."

33

"What?" said Max.

This wasn't making any sense.

The pilot shrugged. "The CASA gave us clearance to land when we filed our original flight plan. But, apparently, a 'very concerned citizen' contacted them a few hours ago and suggested we need to go through a battery of tests to earn our Australian airworthiness certification."

"A guy named Oliver Woodside made the complaint," said the copilot. "Apparently, he's a big muckety-muck here in Australia."

"Yes," said Alexei. "I believe he's the CEO of one of their major oil companies."

"And our former corporate sponsor," said Anna. "I suspect he was out to sabotage our efforts all along."

"He also did a bloomin' great job destroyin' our global reputation," muttered Siobhan. "Ben should've never made a deal with that particular devil."

"He needed the money," said Max, something she never thought she'd have to say about Ben. "He made a mistake."

"Uh, you think?" said Siobhan.

The pilot cleared her throat to refocus everybody's attention to the task at hand. "You guys should make sure your luggage and gear are on that baggage trolley so it can be placed on the correct aircraft for your next flight. Ben's arranged tickets and boarding passes for all of you."

"He wants us to regroup at CMI headquarters," said Charl, reading a text that had just dinged into his device. "We're flying to Israel. Tel Aviv. Then we'll drive to Jerusalem."

Max nodded. When she first joined the CMI, it all started with a flight from New York to Tel Aviv on the way to Jerusalem. It had been her first flight ever.

"Wait a second," she said, turning to the pilot and copilot. "If you two are leaving, how will Ben ever fly his solar-powered jet back to America or Israel or wherever it's supposed to go?"

"No idea," said the pilot. "But Joe and I were just informed our services are no longer required. In fact, Ben just fired us. We're heading home." She held up her boarding pass. "Guess this is our severance package."

"More news," said Isabl, looking up from her phone where she'd just read another incoming text. "Ben has sold the solar-powered jet to someone in Silicon Valley. Says he needed to raise cash to finance our next operation."

"And what, exactly, is that?" said Klaus with an exasperated sigh. "What are we going to find in Jerusalem to spray up into the clouds? Hummus? Falafel balls?"

"Ben didn't elaborate," said Isabl, drily. "But he wants us all to fly there, ASAP. Make sure your bags are on that luggage cart. Then we need to head inside to the terminal. Find our first flights."

"Our *first* flights?" grumbled Siobhan.

"It will take us at least thirty-two hours with three or more stops to reach Jerusalem."

Siobhan rolled her eyes. "Oh, joy. Fine mess you've gotten us into this time, Max."

Max turned to Alexei and Anna. "Look, I know you guys are new, but trust me: this CMI project isn't going the way they usually do."

Anna smirked. "How nice. You guys saved the royal screwup for us."

Totally demoralized, Max and the others tossed their few bags and belongings into the luggage container. Max and Klaus powered down Leo and gently slid him inside his foam-lined, hard-shell travel case. It looked like a giant jelly bean.

When the last piece of cargo was loaded, the man behind the wheel of the tug tapped down on his accelerator. The electric cart whirred away, dragging the rattling trolley to the airport terminal.

As he drove, the man behind the wheel tapped his earpiece and dictated a text to his phone.

"Oni yedut v Iyerusalim cherez Tel'-Aviv."

When Dr. Ivanovich received the message, he, of course, knew exactly what the man had said in Russian: "They are on their way to Jerusalem by way of Tel Aviv."

From a second text, he also learned what time Max's flight would be arriving in Israel.

The trip from Australia to Israel would be so long, Dr. Ivanovich had plenty of time to alert and position his recently contracted operative in Tel Aviv.

His highly trained assassin would be waiting for Max.

34

Max found a seat on the plane that would fly her, Alexei, Siobhan, and Charl from Cairns to Brisbane, the first leg of their four-leg journey.

With more stops in Dubai and Athens, it would take more than forty hours for them to reach Tel Aviv. Nearly two whole days.

Because seats were scarce on such short notice, Klaus, Anna, and Isabl would be taking a different, later flight. Leo would be riding in the cargo hold of their aircraft. This time, it wasn't his choice.

"Let's just hope none of these different airlines we have to take lose our luggage!" Klaus had whined.

When Max and her half of the team boarded their next plane in Brisbane, a lot of the passengers (especially the ones glued to their seat-back TVs) recognized her from all the news coverage of the big cloud-brightening demonstration over the Great Barrier Reef. Some pointed. Some snickered. Some laughed out loud.

"Don't worry about them," Alexei said over his shoulder as they shuffled their way up the narrow aisle to the rear of the cabin.

"Guess they thought the story we were telling was supposed to be funny," said Max.

"It wasn't your fault, Max," said Alexei. "And it definitely wasn't your idea."

She nodded. "I think I'm going to stick to physics and quantum theory from now on."

"Please don't," said Alexei, turning around and smiling. "The world still needs your brain. Big-time."

His cheeks dimpled when he smiled. Max was about to smile back when someone in the row behind her shouted, "So, do you have your jet-powered spray can with you, Little Miss Einstein? Because I forgot to pack my raincoat!"

Alexei closed his eyes and shook his head as he shuffled into his row.

He had a middle seat. So did Max. So did Charl and Siobhan. Fortunately, Charl's seat was right behind Max's. All it took was one "That'll be enough of that" from him to silence all the snickering, giggling, and pointing passengers for the entire fourteen-and-a-half-hour flight from Brisbane to Dubai.

Flying allowed Max's mind to wander. First to Einstein's theory of relativity. Because she saw a fly zigzagging around the cabin. From Max's perspective, the fly was moving at about five miles per hour. A leisurely pace. Sometimes drifting toward the front of the plane, sometimes zipping toward the back.

But Max knew that if someone on the ground (or, in this case, on a boat in the Indian Ocean) had an X-ray telescope and could see through the Emirates airline jet's fuselage, they would observe the insect flying forward at Mach 0.85 (the A380 aircraft's cruising speed) plus five miles per hour—or 657.18 miles per hour.

Speed was relative, depending on how and where you observed it. Every time she saw a fly flitting around inside a moving object she thought about Albert Einstein and his theory of relativity.

Could time be the same?

Max pulled out her journal and started doodling. One way to forget about the humiliation of the cloud-brightening disaster was to exercise her brain in what Einstein called a thought experiment. You didn't need a lab or equipment. You just needed to noodle things out in your head.

How could she do what she was pretty sure her parents had done all those years ago back in Princeton, New Jersey?

How could she use the theory of special relativity to time-travel?

And not just forward. Max wanted to go backward! All the way to 1921. She wanted to reclaim her childhood. To live the life she was supposed to live as Dorothy—daughter of the brilliant Princeton professors Susan and Timothy.

She wanted to be with them when they served orange cake and strawberries to a special visitor. The real Albert Einstein.

But then Max thought about what the late Stephen Hawking (another Einstein-level genius) had said about time travel.

He spoke at a symposium in 2012 and said to the crowd, "I have experimental evidence that time travel is not possible." He told them he had organized a party for time travelers but sent out the invitations *after* the date of the party. "I sat there a long time," he said, "but no one came."

Max closed her journal and closed her eyes.

Okay. If she couldn't go all the way back to 1921, how about last Tuesday? Before she flew to Australia. Before she sprayed the clouds with salt water from seventy-two turbine-powered spritzing machines. It was such a colossal mistake to make such a big deal out of the demonstration. Their failure could derail other young thinkers' ingenious global warming solutions for years. And, by then, it might be too late.

"Don't be so hard on yourself, Max," said the gentle grandfatherly voice of the Einstein in her head. "In science, and in life, we often get things wrong many times before we finally get them right. Especially when you are trying something new."

"I guess," Max muttered, still feeling sorry for herself.

"Max, when you are trying to do something no one else has ever done, how can you possibly know if you've done it correctly? By definition, there is nothing old for you to measure your new idea against. We've all made mistakes. My most famous equation, $E=mc^2$, at first only worked for a particle at rest. Somebody else had to come along and fix my math so it would also work for a particle *in motion*."

"Really?"

"As I said, we all make mistakes, Max. In fact, a person who never made a mistake is a person who never tried anything new."

Max nodded. She liked that.

"And Max?"

"Yes?"

"No matter what the internet might tell you, I didn't say that when I was alive. But you know what?"

"What?"

"I wish I had."

35

Nearly two full days after the cloud-brightening debacle in Australia, Max and her half of the team arrived at Ben Gurion Airport in Tel Aviv, Israel.

Everyone was exhausted. Jet-lagged.

So the forty-minute drive into Jerusalem, home to the CMI headquarters (not to mention the Albert Einstein Archives on the Givat Ram campus of Hebrew University), was unusually quiet.

Maybe because Klaus was still in the air with Anna and Isabl. Klaus did most of the yakking on group road trips. Maybe because Max, Charl, Alexei, and Siobhan were crammed into the cramped confines of an airport taxi van.

Everybody was trying hard not to breathe through their noses. Because none of them had bathed or showered or even used deodorant for two whole days.

Max barely noticed the glittering Dome of the Rock or the Citadel, which Charl had called the Tower of David when Max made her first journey to Jerusalem to join the CMI. When exactly was that? So much had happened since, it felt like a decade ago.

The taxi van dropped Max and the group off in front of a nondescript, all-glass modern building near the downtown triangle in the western part of the city. Its mirrored walls helped it blend in with all the office buildings surrounding it.

This was CMI headquarters. This was where Max took the tests and tolerated the interview process that made her the leader of Ben Abercrombie's do-gooding band of young geniuses. This was where Max Einstein was first called "The Chosen One." But, after the public humiliation in the land down under, she wondered if her new title should be "The Ridiculous One." Or maybe just "The Fool."

Max led the way into the building. Charl brought up the rear, all the while scanning the sidewalk and street for any signs of trouble.

Keeto, Tisa, and Vihaan were hanging out in the lobby. None of them would make eye contact with Max, Siobhan, or Alexei. Finally, Vihaan spoke.

"We're so sorry for how the media portrayed what appeared to be a very successful attempt at cloud brightening."

"You're not a silly little girl," said Tisa.

"Excuse me?" said Max.

"That's what some oil company guy called you on CNN," explained Keeto. "Dude needs an attitude adjustment."

"Where's Ben?" asked Charl, after checking to make sure the entrance doors were secure.

"At his hotel," said Vihaan.

"The King David?" said Max, assuming Ben would be staying at one of the most luxurious five-star hotels in the city.

Tisa shook her head. "No. He's at a youth hostel."

"What?" blurted Siobhan.

Tisa shrugged. "He's on a tight budget. I guess we all are."

"Why don't you guys take your bags to your rooms?" Charl suggested.

"Our old rooms?" asked Max.

Charl nodded. "Alexei? You're new. I'll show you where you'll be bunking. Everybody from my flight? Grab a little shut-eye. We need you fresh and your minds sharp. We'll meet in the auditorium at nineteen-hundred hours. Ben will be here. So will Isabl, Klaus, and Anna. Ben's going to talk about our next big thing."

A lot of eyebrows were raised when Max and the others heard that. *Hadn't the last big thing been a big enough disaster for Ben?*

Max grabbed her small duffel, said good-bye to her friends, and shuffled off to her old room.

As she made her way down the darkened corridor, she noticed a framed photograph on the wall. It was lopsided, so she straightened it. A brass plaque on the frame identified the group in the picture as THE FIRST CMI TEAM.

Max remembered posing for the picture, right after she had "won" the competition to lead the group. Everybody was smiling. Except Klaus. He was sort of smirking. Max noticed that the photo had started to fade. The picture frame's glass was smudged with dirt. She studied the faces of the players who were no longer on the CMI team. Hana, the vegan botanist. Ms. Kaplan, the stern disciplinarian who had administered the tests Max had hated so much.

Ms. Kaplan turned out to be a spy. Hana turned into a turncoat.

As she continued down the hall, Max couldn't help but notice how run-down the whole place felt. Gone was all the former bustle and excitement. What remained was a musty shell. An empty building without a pulse.

Now Max saw a lopsided switch plate, its screws loose.

So when did Ben fire the custodial crew? she wondered. The place looked like a dump. She pulled her Swiss Army knife out of her pocket, flipped open the screwdriver tool, straightened and tightened the switch plate. It was a small fix. Maybe if she had a week or two, she could make the whole building look and feel better.

But now she needed to flop down on a bed and sleep. The trip from Australia had been exhausting.

She needed to be ready for whatever "next big thing" Ben was cooking up.

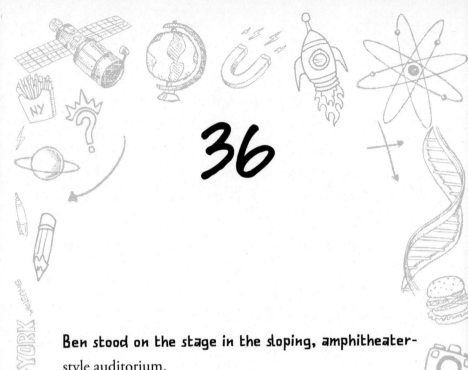

36

Ben stood on the stage in the sloping, amphitheater-style auditorium.

He was bathed in a spotlight.

Totally unlike him, thought Max. She knew Ben to be shy and socially awkward. Ben Abercrombie would rather look down at his shoelaces than look you in the eye. He had never craved the spotlight. Now he was literally standing in one.

Only the first two rows of the one-hundred-seat auditorium were filled. Max sat between Alexei and Tisa. Everybody else was there, too: Siobhan, Keeto, Toma, Vihaan,

Klaus, Annika, Charl, and Isabl. The only one missing was Leo. His travel case was somewhere in Dubai. Or Athens. Or maybe he'd been put on a flight to London or New York or Paris. The airlines weren't sure. But they were working on it.

"I, uh, know some of you have suggested that we should run a new series of tests," Ben said, pushing his glasses up the bridge of his nose with his forefinger. "That we should bring in the psychologists and have a whole host of new interviews."

Max looked to Tisa. She shrugged. Tisa had no idea what Ben was talking about, either.

"That, after what happened down in Australia, we should replace Max as our chosen one."

Oh-kay, thought Max. Someone wanted her title. Well, as far as she was concerned, they could have it.

Now Ben consulted a bright-yellow note card. "It has also been suggested that our two newcomers, Anna and Alexei, should be removed from the CMI team because, and I quote, 'neither one of them is a scientist or half as smart as me.' Thank you, Klaus, for that input."

Everybody turned to glare at Klaus.

"Hey," he said defensively, "your stupid cloud-brightening 'story' idea made us the laughingstock of the world and ended with one of the airlines I had to take to get here losing our robot."

"It wasn't our idea to brighten the clouds over the Great Barrier Reef," said Anna.

"Or to sign on with an oil company as a cosponsor," added Alexei.

"These guys were just trying to do the best with what they were given," said Max.

"And it cost us Leo!" said Klaus. "I should be the new chosen one."

"That doesn't make logical sense, Klaus," said Annika. "One statement does not support the other..."

"Plus, you were totally uncool on camera," Keeto told Klaus. "Making jokes about what everybody else was trying to do? Totally. Uncool."

"I think maybe Vihaan should be in charge," said Tisa, much to Max's surprise. "After all, he managed the water project in India all by himself."

Now Siobhan, Max's other best friend at CMI, was nodding her head. "Good on you, Tisa. Smart idea. Vihaan should take over."

"I don't care," huffed Klaus. "It doesn't have to be me. It just can't be Max Einstein anymore. She has done a terrible job. We lost a robot, people!"

"We'll find Leo," said Max.

"How?"

"Was there a baggage sticker on his travel crate?" asked Vihaan. "Those are computer coded and—"

"Doesn't matter!" snapped Klaus. "It could've fallen off."

"We did have to change planes three different times," said Anna.

"You should've bought Leo his own ticket," suggested Keeto. "Let him ride in coach with you guys."

And then the whole auditorium erupted into an angry barrage of accusations. The CMI team didn't sound like a team anymore. They sounded like a squabbling family on the worst day of a rainy summer vacation.

Finally, Charl and Isabl stood up.

"Knock it off!" boomed Isabl.

"Remember who you are!" added Charl.

"A bunch of losers," muttered Klaus.

"I am going to make a change," said Ben, after taking a deep, steadying breath. "Max? You're no longer the chosen one. Sorry."

Max gave him a "Hey, it's fine by me" shoulder shrug. Because it was fine by her.

"Who's taking her place?" asked Annika.

Ben adjusted his glasses some more.

And then he said, "Me."

37

The room went silent.

Finally, Siobhan piped up. "Seriously? You?"

"Yes," said Ben, clearing his throat and standing a little straighter. "Me. I am officially choosing myself to be the chosen one."

"Um, shouldn't you have to take all those tests we had to take first?" said Keeto. "Maybe talk to that creepy shrink?"

"No. This is my Change Makers Institute. I can do as I think best. Now then, I am eager for us all to move forward. What happened in Australia was a mistake. I'll admit that. But only because it wasn't big or bold enough."

Suddenly, there was a noise outside the auditorium doors. A shattering of glass.

Had someone broken into the headquarters building?

"You guys stay here," said Charl.

"We're on it," said Isabl.

The two commandos scurried out of the auditorium.

"We're fine," said Ben. "Charl and Isabl will take care of, uh, whatever needs to be taken care of. I will now, you know, proceed with my presentation..."

Hand trembling slightly, he pushed a button on a remote control. The lights in the auditorium dimmed. A video screen scrolled down behind him. A few seconds later, the screen erupted with the violent images of soot clouds billowing out of a volcanic crater.

"This is Mount Pinatubo in the Philippines," said Ben. "The world's largest volcanic eruption in the past one hundred years. Gas-charged magma exploded into an umbrella of ash clouds that rose as high as nineteen kilometers. That's nearly twelve miles. That ash shrouded the earth in a massive cloud of sulfur dioxide gas that spiraled up into the stratosphere where it combined with hydrogen to create fine droplets of powder called aerosols that reflected enough sunlight back into space to cool the earth's surface by nearly one degree Fahrenheit. The Mount Pinatubo cooling lasted for almost a year. So, I've been thinking.

Doing what Albert Einstein would call a thought experiment. What if there was a way to inject the stratosphere with sulfur dioxide without a volcano?"

Max slumped down in her seat as Ben outlined his next big idea. It involved a fleet of jets or weather balloons or even a space shuttle flying at an extreme altitude of seventy thousand feet where they would crop dust the stratosphere with a sulfur compound.

"Geoscientists call this 'stratospheric aerosol injection.'"

"We do," said Siobhan from somewhere in the darkened row behind Max.

"It would cool the earth and give us some absolutely fantastic sunsets," Ben continued.

Ben's losing it, Max thought. *He is out to lunch. Something is seriously wrong.*

She turned to see if Alexei agreed that Ben had gone off the rails.

But Alexei wasn't sitting next to Max anymore.

She looked around.

She saw him. Up near the top of the seats. Silhouetted against a dim sliver of light.

He was carefully easing open an exit door and sneaking out of the auditorium.

How to inject sulfur dioxide into the air without a volcano:

38

Max remembered her first trip to Jerusalem and what it felt like to be the new kid joining the CMI.

She'd basically quit and sneaked out of the building like Alexei had just done.

Alexei was probably feeling the same feels Max had felt back then. He was probably wondering what he had signed up for. Who were these so-called geniuses and why were they spraying salt water at clouds or trying to re-create volcanic ash at an altitude of seventy thousand feet? Those kinds of science-fiction stories might not be the kind Alexei wanted to tell.

Max remembered what Alexei had told her before they

visited the green roof on top of the convention center in New York City. *"There are so many simpler solutions. They make good stories, too...if not good TV."*

Max had been lucky when she'd angrily stomped out of the CMI headquarters fuming. Isabl had immediately come looking for her. And, of course, being some kind of ex-military specialist, Isabl had also immediately found Max. Then she had quoted some Einstein: "The world is more threatened by those who tolerate evil or support it than the evildoers themselves."

If there was going to be a change for good in the world, people would have to stand up against all the evil.

That was really all it had taken. Max was back on board.

But Charl and Isabl had already left the auditorium, trying to figure out what that smashed glass was all about. *Was somebody (probably somebody Russian) trying to break into the CMI building? Was Alexei in danger?*

The security team probably hadn't even seen Alexei leave. They couldn't track him down and quote Einstein at him.

But Max could.

So while Ben kept going through his PowerPoint presentation about injecting a million tons of sulfur dioxide into the stratosphere, she crouched low and tiptoed past the empty seats in her row, into the aisle, and out an exit.

Nobody saw her. Nobody heard her leave.

Max hurried up the circular corridor, noticing a shattered picture frame on the floor. Its mounting hook had come loose from the wall. The heavy thing had fallen. There was no need for an intruder alert. Just some better building maintenance.

Max wanted to find Charl and Isabl and show them what she'd discovered so they could stand down.

But she saw Alexei outside. In front of the building. Kicking at some pebbles on the sidewalk.

Max knew she shouldn't leave the building. Not without her security detail. But she often did stuff people told her she shouldn't do. She pushed open the front door and stepped outside.

"Hey," she said to Alexei.

"Hey," he said back.

Max gestured over her shoulder. "Not what you signed on for, huh?"

"Sorry," said Alexei.

That confused Max a little. "Sorry? For what?"

"Everything."

That's when Max saw a gaunt man in a business suit carrying an umbrella—even though there wasn't a cloud in the bright-blue sky. The man's skin was so tight and shiny on his bony face that it looked like a polished skull.

"Zdravstvuyte, Aleksey," the man said with a sinister smile.

Alexei gave the man his boyish grin. *"Zdravstvuyte. Kak ty uznal moye imya?"*

They were speaking Russian!

Just like the commandos who dropped out of the attack helicopter over the Jacob K. Javits Convention Center in New York City.

When Max and Alexei were also alone.

Was that what Alexei was so sorry about? That he was another mole, secretly working undercover for whomever the Russian people were who wanted Max dead? Was his assignment to lure Max into compromised situations? To get her alone and unprotected so they could strike?

The gaunt man stepped forward, jauntily raising the tip of his umbrella. *"Prekrasnyy u nas den', soglasny?"* he said, smiling his thin-lipped death mask smile.

"Watch out, Max," said Alexei, putting himself between Max and the umbrella. "That could be what they call a Bulgarian umbrella. A weapon with a poison pellet in the tip!"

The gaunt man chuckled. "Silly boy," he said in heavily accented English. "You watch too many spy movies."

Max probably did, too. She recognized the umbrella for what it was. An ingeniously engineered dart gun!

Suddenly, the man lunged forward, aiming his umbrella like a fencing foil at Max.

Alexei leapt up, twirled around, and swung his left leg into a flying back kick. His foot connected with the umbrella below the tip and sent it skittering into the middle of the street.

Furious, the gaunt man found his footing and pulled out a very angry-looking knife. He made a move to slash at Alexei.

Which Alexei countered by springing into another kick. This one was a front push kick, placing the heel of his right foot all the way up in the man's jutting chin. Stunned, the man's eyes bulged. The knife clattered to the concrete. The man lost his balance, flew backward, and ended up sprawled in the gutter.

"Run!" shouted Alexei. "Run!"

He and Max did.

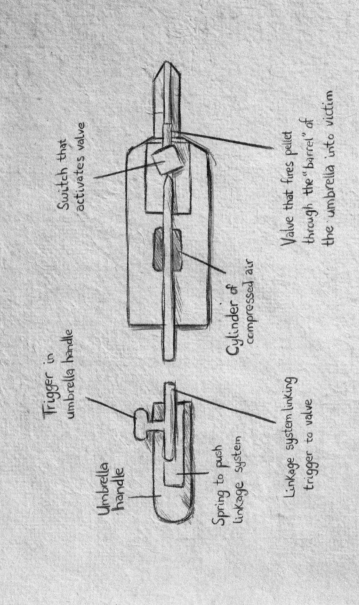

Switch that activates valve

Valve that fires pellet through the "barrel" of the umbrella into victim

Cylinder of compressed air

Trigger in umbrella handle

Linkage system linking trigger to valve

Umbrella handle

Spring to push linkage system

39

Max and Alexei had about a minute head start on the gaunt man sitting in the gutter rubbing his chin.

Max glanced over her shoulder and saw him struggling to his feet. Max whipped her head back around to see if there was someplace she and Alexei could hide.

Because the man with the poison-tipped umbrella was relentless.

He dashed into traffic to retrieve his weapon. He'd soon be charging up the sidewalk behind them.

"In there!" Max shouted, seeing the service entrance to a hotel kitchen.

A sign on the door said the hotel's restaurant was closed for remodeling. Fortunately, the door was unlocked.

"Hotel lobbies are filled with people," Max said to Alexei as they raced past industrial-grade appliances and stainless-steel racks filled with heavy pots and pans. They made it to the door where the kitchen opened into the restaurant. Max figured the hotel restaurant would be right off the people-packed hotel lobby and provide relative safety.

She tugged on the door.

This one was locked.

Because the restaurant is closed for repairs! Duh.

"Now what?" asked Alexei, keeping his cool. "I suspect our Russian friend saw us duck into that doorway."

Max nodded. "Yeah. He looked like a pro. Pros notice stuff like that. So how'd he know your name?"

Alexei gave her a look that said, *"Really? You want to talk about that now?"*

"Hey, it's like you said, Max. The guy's a pro. Means he does his homework. He probably knows all our names!"

Max scanned the kitchen for a hiding place. They were both too big to climb into the ovens. The open shelves, even the ones loaded with huge, dented pots, wouldn't provide much cover. And then she saw the shimmering stainless-steel door to a massive walk-in freezer.

"There!" she said.

"Max?" Alexei whispered tensely. "It's a freezer."

"Maybe they shut it off during renovations."

"Maybe they didn't. Maybe it'll be minus ten degrees inside."

"Which is why that madman with the lethal umbrella will never suspect that we'd hide in there."

Alexei grinned a little. "I thought you were supposed to be super smart."

"Sorry," said Max. "We're all out of options. It's either the freezer or you do some more tae kwon do on the guy." She led the way to the walk-in freezer wall. "By the way, where'd you learn to fight like that? I thought you were more of a poet. Why'd you wait so long to show me your karate skills?"

"Because, Max, I believe that violence should always be the last resort. And it's systema. Not tae kwon do or karate. *Systema*. Old-school Soviet-style self-defense."

"Which means our attacker probably knows it, too!"

Alexei thought about that for half a second. "Hiding inside the freezer sounds like an excellent plan."

They hurried into the metal cabinet and pulled the door shut tight behind them.

The freezer wasn't switched off for the renovations. It was bone-chillingly cold inside the frigid box. The stainless-steel walls were coated with frost. Max thought her nose might snap off her face like an icicle.

Ten seconds later, Max heard the service door to the street burst open.

Heavy boots clicked across the floor.

"Where are you?" shouted the very angry man in his stilted English. "I know you two are being in here! Alexei? We do not wish to harm you, comrade. Give us Max Einstein. *Sdelay eto dlya matushki Rossii.*"

Max turned to Alexei. He looked spooky, illuminated by the single bare bulb caged in the middle of the walk-in freezer's ceiling. He was hugging himself and shivering. His breath came out in rapid puffs of steam. He shook his head.

"Don't worry," he mouthed. "We'll be fine. I'm not turning you over to 'Mother Russia.'"

The handle on the freezer door rattled. The man had clearly figured out where they were hiding. He shook the handle hard. The door rocked a little. But it did not swing open.

Then the man stopped trying to force open the door. Instead, he laughed.

"And I heard you were very smart, Max Einstein. Too bad you foolish children decided to hide inside a freezer with a broken lock. I cannot open it from out here. You cannot open it from in there. Perhaps this lock will be the first thing they will repair when they remodel the kitchen. Anyway, this is good. I can save my dart for some other day. I do not need to waste my precious poison on you two. The freezer will kill you soon enough. *Do svidaniya, Aleksey.* So long, Max."

Max and Alexei remained still and quiet (except for the chattering of their teeth). They could hear boot heels shuffling across the kitchen floor. The man was leaving. He was also still laughing.

Because he was right.

He didn't need to kill Max and Alexei anymore.

The freezer would do his job for him.

40

Max and Alexei were trapped.

Blood boiling, no matter how cold it was inside the freezer, Max gave Alexei a dirty look.

"I'll ask again: How did he know your name? Did you set me up?"

"No, Max," said Alexei, who was hugging himself and stamping his feet in an effort to stay warm. "That's why when he said 'Hello, Alexei,' in Russian, I said *'Kak ty uznal moye imya.'* Loose translation? 'How do you know my name?' I was as surprised as you were. But now we're trapped inside a metal box where it's minus ten degrees. We need to call Charl and Isabl!"

He pulled out his phone. He jabbed at the glass face. It wouldn't work.

"The rapid drop in temperature from out there to in here caused moisture to condense inside the cavities of your phone," Max explained as her eyes swept the interior of the walk-in freezer to assess their situation. "Eventually, those condensed water particles will freeze and expand inside your phone. Everything will become brittle. Water's the only liquid that expands when it freezes. Pretty soon, that expansion will put so much pressure on your phone, the whole thing will crack open."

"Guess I sh-sh-should've signed up for th-th-the ph-ph-phone insurance p-p-plan." The cold was starting to get to him. Max's brain was racing so fast, the adrenaline was keeping her warm.

She took another look around the small, icy room.

And then her eyes lit up the way they always did when she had a lightning strike of inspiration.

"Of course!" she said.

"Of c-c-course what?" said Alexei.

"There's a way to get out of here."

She took a quick inventory of what she had to work with. Some cardboard cartons of frozen food. Several plastic bags of ice cubes. A rack system hanging overhead. That naked light bulb inside its metal cage.

She might be able to "Apollo 13" their predicament, she thought, remembering the greatest space hack of all time, when the crew of the seemingly doomed Apollo 13 flight had to use whatever they had on hand—like duct tape and tube socks—to repair their spacecraft after an oxygen tank exploded.

She built a stepstool out of the frozen food cartons and slid them to the center of the room, positioning the stack right underneath the caged light bulb.

"Break up the ice cubes in one of those plastic bags," she told Alexei as she climbed up on the cardboard tower and swung open the cage protecting the naked light bulb.

"Ouch!"

The metal was hot.

That was a good thing. An excellent thing.

Next, Max pulled out her Swiss Army knife and used a blade and screwdriver attachment to remove one of the metal bars suspended from the ceiling. She figured it was probably for hanging meat. Fortunately, the restaurant was closed so there weren't any heavy slabs of beef to deal with.

"Perfect," Max said, studying the metal bar. "It has a groove."

"So?" said Alexei, who was repeatedly dropping a five-pound sack of ice on the freezer floor to break up the clumped-together cubes.

"So it will work like a rain gutter and channel the water to where we want it to go."

"And where's that?"

"The lock. Remember what I said about water expanding when it freezes? Well, if it can crack open your phone, it can also crack open the lock. Hand me a bunch of those ice cubes."

Alexei did. Max stuffed them (temporarily) into her pocket. Her legs were already so cold, a fistful of ice cubes wasn't going to make them feel any worse.

"I'll melt the ice up here with heat from this light bulb. You position the other end of this metal bar so the water runs down and dribbles into the lock. At minus ten, it'll refreeze in a flash."

"You really are a genius," said Alexei, taking his end of the metal channel and propping it up against the freezer door's lock.

"Thanks," said Max. "I guess I just like stories with happy endings."

"And lots of ch-ch-chilling suspense," joked Alexei.

Max laughed a little. She'd laugh more if this lock-cracking hack really worked.

She held a fistful of ice cubes close to the light bulb. They began to melt. The water slid down the chute. It seeped into the door lock.

"Time to reload," she said.

Alexei rested the lip of the metal bar on the door handle so he could run back to the ice cube bag and hand Max some more solidified water.

After three loads of melted ice, the runoff was enough to completely fill the lock's mechanical chamber.

Then all they had to do was wait. For the water to freeze. For the inner workings of the lock to become brittle.

It didn't take very long.

They heard crackling and snapping.

"Stand back," said Alexei.

He gave the door another one of his martial arts kicks.

The lock popped. The door swung open freely. When Max and Alexei stepped into the kitchen, Charl and Isabl had just stormed in.

Charl was holding an umbrella.

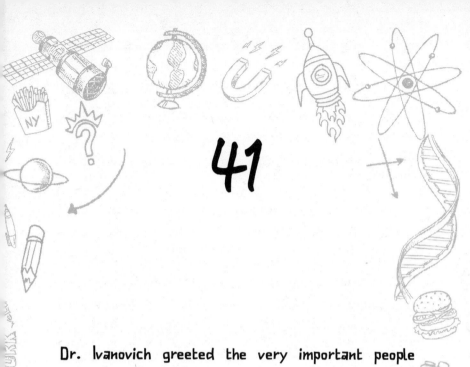

41

Dr. Ivanovich greeted the very important people assembled in his hotel suite with a series of polite head nods.

If he shook hands, he wouldn't be able to fidget with the clacking pair of diamonds he rolled around in his right palm.

"What is that you are fiddling with, Herr Doktor?" asked an elegant Swiss banker with swept-back white hair.

"Compressed carbon," Dr. Ivanovich said with a thin smile. "Please. Enjoy some light refreshments."

Dr. Ivanovich gestured to the elegant buffet table set up in his suite of rooms at the Beau-Rivage, one of Geneva's most luxurious and distinguished hotels. The Beau-Rivage

207

also had a reputation for discretion. Which made it ideal for the extremely secretive Okamenelosti Group's intimate gathering in the shadow of the Swiss Alps. "The Fossils" didn't want anyone telling the world what they were up to.

Or that they even existed.

Dr. Ivanovich had come to Geneva to meet with the bankers (from all around the globe) that his organization had helped make rich with oil money. This early spring get-together was his way of reminding the powerful money men and women that, unlike most banking transactions, *they* owed *him*. Their bank vaults would not be filled to overflowing if not for the steady stream of petrodollars flowing from the Fossils and their oil interests.

Someday, those debts would come due.

"Doctor?" His personal assistant, Vlad, came to where Dr. Ivanovich stood studying his guests as they mingled and drank the hotel's most expensive champagne while nibbling on a host of dainty hors d'oeuvres. "I hate to disturb you, sir..."

Ivanovich studied the pained expression on Vlad's face.

"What is it, Vladimir?" asked Dr. Ivanovich, tumbling the twin diamonds in his clenched fist a little faster.

"Pavel failed."

Dr. Ivanovich's eyes narrowed. He did not tolerate failure.

"What happened?" he asked.

"He is currently in the custody of the Israeli intelligence agency."

"Mossad?"

Vlad nodded. "Charl and Isabl, the CMI's security team, apprehended Pavel in Jerusalem. His handler assures us Pavel will not break under interrogation. Besides, we contracted with him through a web of back channels. He has no way of knowing that the Okamenelosti Group were the ones paying his fee."

Dr. Ivanovich moved the diamonds in and out and around his hands. It helped him think. He couldn't care less about their hired assassin Pavel Zakhar Victorovich's current plight. The man and his Bulgarian umbrella were both disposable assets.

But...

The presence of this highly skilled, two-person CMI security team was making reaching and eliminating Max Einstein far more difficult.

Maybe even impossible.

It was time to switch to Plan B.

B as in Bankers. All those debts owed to Dr. Ivanovich had just come due. It was time to collect payment in full.

"Excuse me, Vlad. I must talk with a few of our distinguished guests."

"Of course, Dr. Ivanovich. But shall I make inquiries? Find another... expediter? Will we be renewing our efforts to remove the threat posed by Max Einstein?"

"Yes. But, this time, she will not be our target."

Vlad looked surprised by that answer. "I see. Who then?"

"Young Mr. Benjamin Franklin Abercrombie, of course. The so-called Benefactor financing the CMI."

Vlad looked around. Lowered his voice. "Shall I initiate contact with other contract killers, sir?"

Dr. Ivanovich's smile widened.

"No, Vlad. We're not going to kill young Benjamin." Now Ivanovich actually laughed. "But, when we are finished with him, he may very well wish we had."

42

"Your assailant was Pavel Zakhar Victorovich," Charl told Max and Alexei.

He said it very calmly, because that's how he said everything.

"He is also known by his Russian nickname, Cherep," added Isabl.

"The skull," said Alexei, translating.

Charl nodded. "Correct. He is one of the most ruthless and cunning hired assassins currently operating in the dark world of black ops mercenaries. The Israeli intelligence agency was extremely delighted to take him off our hands."

"Our friends with Mossad alerted us about his presence

in the vicinity of CMI headquarters," Isabl explained. "About ten seconds after we realized that you two had gone missing."

Charl was still holding the umbrella. It was slightly bent. Dented from where Alexei had kicked it.

"We need to turn that over to Mossad," Isabl told him.

"We will," said Charl. "I just wanted Max and Alexei to see how close they came to getting killed."

Charl pointed the umbrella toward the floor and depressed the trigger in the handle.

There was a sharp, soft *THWICK* as a tiny pellet shot out of the tip.

Max and Alexei instinctively jumped back.

"Don't ever put yourself in that kind of danger again," said Charl.

"You two don't go anywhere—alone or together—without one of us," added Isabl.

"I'm sorry," said Alexei. "It was my fault. Max only came outside to check on me."

"Quick question," said Max, with a slight shiver. (For some reason, now that they were out of the freezer, she suddenly felt cold.) "Did this Pavel Zakhar Victorovich guy have a nasty bruise on his bony chin?"

"Yes," said Isabl. "Why?"

Max nodded to Alexei. "Because our high-kicking humanist here put it there."

"I have a little training in the martial arts," Alexei said, humbly.

"A little?" said Max. "You were awesome."

"So were you. That thing with the ice and the lock inside the deep freeze? Genius. You saved our lives with your brain."

Max gave a coy grin and a shrug as if to say, "Genius is what I do best."

Charl glanced at his watch. "We need to head back. Ben's still making his presentation."

"Um, could you guys give us a second?" Max asked Charl and Isabl. "There's something I need to say to Alexei. In private."

"We'll be right outside that door," said Charl.

Charl and Isabl stepped out of the kitchen and onto the sidewalk. They left the door open. Apparently, they didn't totally trust Max and Alexei not to do anything dumb. Again.

Max turned to Alexei. "I'm sorry."

"For what? The freezer idea? It was actually an excellent hiding place. Probably our only option."

"No, I'm sorry for thinking that you were somehow involved in setting me up for attacks by scary Russians."

"Hey, I would've thought the same thing. First the roof garden on top of the Javits Center. Now here? There've been far too many scary Russian guys mysteriously appearing whenever you're alone with this scary Russian guy."

"You're not scary," said Max. "Well, your kicks are, but you aren't."

The butterflies were back in her stomach. Alexei's sparkling eyes seemed to have turned a bluer shade of blue.

"So, should we head back?" she said. "Hear what Ben has to say about crop dusting the stratosphere with sulfur?"

"I'd rather not," said Alexei. "Going big isn't the only solution to the global warming crisis. There are so many small steps we could take, Max. Like, I don't know, meatless Mondays. That's where you decide to be vegetarian one night a week. Sure, it's a small step, but it would have an impact if everybody did it. Did you know that meat production makes more greenhouse gases than all the planes, trains, and cars in the world combined?"

Max did not know that.

"Don't tell Klaus," she joked. "He loves his sausages."

"If I did tell him, he'd just tell me it was a hoax. Or bad science. Or an urban myth."

"My hero Albert Einstein became a vegetarian. Of

course, it was late in his life. And he mostly did it for medical reasons, but still..."

Charl and Isabl came back into the kitchen.

"Sorry," said Max. "Guess we took longer than a second..."

Isabl held up her phone. "Ben just texted. He wants us back in the auditorium with the others. ASAP. There's some kind of emergency."

"What?" said Alexei. "NASA won't let him borrow their space shuttle to dump sulfur in the stratosphere?"

Max heard Charl and Isabl's phones both ding with what was probably a second text. Hers might've given her an alert, too, if it hadn't died along with Alexei's in the deep freeze.

Charl and Isabl stared at their phone screens for what seemed like hours. (More proof of Einstein's theory of relativity: time always slowed down whenever you wanted it to speed up.)

"Impossible," muttered Isabl.

"What?" said Max. "What's impossible?"

"Ben. He's going to shut down the CMI. His money is all gone. There won't be any more missions."

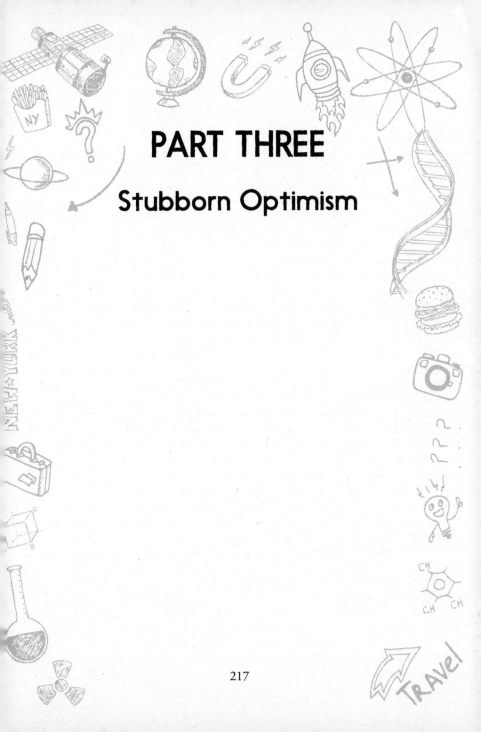

PART THREE

Stubborn Optimism

43

"Um, there's been some...irregularities."

Head down and shoulders slumped, Ben stood on the dimly lit stage at CMI headquarters, struggling to read what he'd written out on a sheet of paper. The paper rattled in his hands as his whole body seemed to tremble. Max's heart was breaking for the poor guy.

"It's, uh, my bank accounts. All of them. Well, most of them. Okay, enough of them. I guess I spent too much on the solar-powered jet. And the cloud-brightening project in Australia. And everything else. Because I am wiped out. All my money and all my family's money is gone..."

When he looked up, Max could see that his eyes were damp. It was taking everything Ben had not to cry.

The whole team was assembled in the front rows of the auditorium. This unlikely assortment of international geniuses and global prodigies had become, for the most part, a pretty happy family. Even Klaus. He was like everybody's oafish brother. Sure, he could be a pain sometimes, but he was family.

Now Ben was, basically, saying that the family was breaking up.

"There will be no more missions. No more CMI. In fact, my, uh, creditors have requested that we vacate this building before seven tomorrow morning. So, uh, I suggest you all pack up as quickly as you can. The repo people will be arriving later to haul away most of the furniture and fixtures. My credit cards and bank loans are all being called in..."

His voice trailed off.

"What about Leo?" asked Klaus. His voice was soft and missing its usual bluster. "We need to find Leo."

"I'm sorry," said Ben. "We'll have to leave that to the airlines. We don't have the resources to initiate our own search and recovery mission. We don't have the resources to do anything. Fortunately, all of your tickets for returning home were purchased before this financial disaster took place. Back when we, uh, arranged for your flights to Israel. You can all go home. But, before you do, I just wanted to thank you all for helping make my dream come true. We did a lot of good in the world. But now, well, that dream is over. It's time for me to say good-bye and thank you for all your hard work. I expect great things from all of you in the future."

And, with that, Ben tucked his sheet of paper into a pocket and silently strolled out of the room.

After Ben made his somber exit, the ten young geniuses— as well as Charl and Isabl—sat in stunned silence.

Which Klaus, of course, broke.

"Seriously? That's it?"

"Don't we even receive any lovely parting gifts?" cracked Keeto. "Some kind of CMI swag? Maybe a water bottle or a baseball cap with a logo on it?"

"I could call my father," offered Tisa. "Maybe he could loan Ben the money he needs to keep going."

Annika shook her head. "That would not be a logical move for your father, Tisa. Then he'd be broke, too."

Max just sat there. Soaking it all in. The grandest adventure of her life was coming to a very unsatisfying end.

"This is like a very terrible movie," said Vihaan. "One where the bad guys win because the movie people ran out of money and couldn't afford to film the happy ending."

"Worst story ever," muttered Alexei.

"Totally off brand," added Anna.

At first, the ten teammates groused and complained and rejected the very idea that the Change Makers Institute would be no more. But, gradually, they started to accept the truth.

It was done. They weren't a team anymore.

"It's time to pack it in and move on," said the ever stoic Charl.

"We had a good run," said Isabl. "You kids were an honor to work with. We wish you well in all that you will, undoubtedly, accomplish."

Charl and Isabl left the auditorium. One good thing about the CMI breaking up? The kids weren't a target any longer. They wouldn't need around-the-clock security and protection.

Finally, it was time for hugs, tears, and good-byes.

Phone numbers were exchanged.

Except, thanks to their time in the deep freeze, Max and Alexei no longer had working phones.

"Here," said Klaus, snapping open an aluminum attaché

case. There were half a dozen high-end devices lined up in foam slots. "Take one of mine."

"How come you have so many phones?" asked an amused Alexei as Klaus programmed a pair of devices, one for Alexei, the other for Max.

Klaus shrugged. "I'm a nerd and a tech geek. Gadgets are what I do best. I'm still working on the whole 'human interaction' thing."

Max smiled and took her new phone. "You're doing pretty good in that department, too, Klaus. And if I hear anything about Leo, I'll definitely give you a call."

Klaus nodded. "Good."

After a couple of hours, just about everyone had caught a taxi to the airport and their return trips home to Ireland, India, China, and elsewhere.

"What's next for you?" Max asked Alexei when they were the only ones still in the lobby of the building.

"I will go home to Russia. And you?"

Max hesitated. She really didn't have an answer.

Because she really didn't have a home.

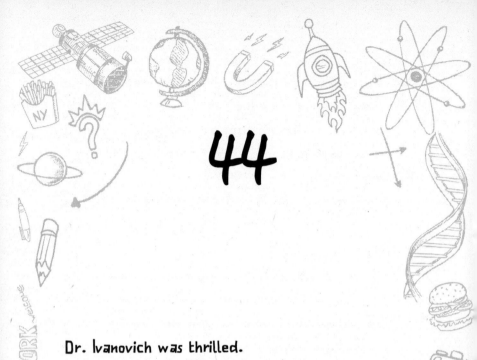

44

Dr. Ivanovich was thrilled.

"My banker friends granted my request," he told the woman accompanying him as he strode down the cobblestone corridors of his mountaintop fortress. "The young prince Benjamin Franklin Abercrombie has just begun his new life as a pauper. All it took was a few taps of an encrypted delete key to wipe out his entire fortune and send him into poverty. All the money he inherited? Poof. It vanished."

"Where did it go?" asked the woman.

Dr. Ivanovich grinned. "Who can say for certain, Ms. Kaplan? These financial matters can be so complicated. So

mysterious. But I did notice a very significant uptick in my own bank accounts late last night..."

The woman walking alongside Dr. Ivanovich was Tari Kaplan, the traitor who had pretended to work for Ben Abercrombie and the CMI while she actually worked for the now-defunct Corp. Ms. Kaplan was the stern matron in Jerusalem who had been so hard on Max Einstein when Max was the last to join the team of young geniuses being assembled to "do good" in the world.

Ms. Kaplan didn't relish the news of Ben's financial demise as much as Dr. Ivanovich clearly did. In truth, she had some regrets. Some remorse. She had never planned to become one with the evil forces out to completely crush the Change Makers Institute.

She just wanted the pushy pretender Max Einstein to be dealt with. Swiftly and severely.

Tari Kaplan never did like the brainy little girl. Not from the first minute she'd heard the girl's name. *(How dare she name herself after the world's greatest genius, Albert Einstein?)* Everything Tari Kaplan had done, she had done to destroy the so-called Chosen One.

And, of course, to make a little money with the Corp.

Money was a good thing. A thing that young Benjamin probably wished he had more of right now.

Ms. Kaplan followed Dr. Ivanovich into a chilly, high-ceilinged stone room. A roll-up steel garage door filled one whole wall. There was the faint odor of diesel fumes from trucks parked outside in the cold. This appeared to be Dr. Ivanovich's shipping and receiving department.

There was an oblong container sitting on the floor with Australian airline tags dangling from its side handles. It looked like a jumbo version of one of those luggage tubes you see strapped to the roof of a car. Or maybe a hard-shelled plastic coffin.

"Open it," Dr. Ivanovich snapped at two paramilitary soldiers in snow camo gear.

"Yes, sir!"

The doctor patiently rolled his clacking diamonds around and around in the palm of his left hand waiting for the two men to pop open several latches and raise the lid on the cargo container.

Ms. Kaplan gasped.

It was Leo. The automaton with the face of a young boy that the Corp had named Lenard was laid out like a corpse in a casket. The robot had been originally designed and programmed to help Dr. Zimm and the Corp destroy Max Einstein. But then the CMI "captured" Lenard and altered his circuits. Thanks to Klaus, the brainy tech wiz, the giggling demon-bot became quite pleasant and extremely resourceful. Another very valuable member of Ben Abercrombie's young team.

"Our man on the ground in Australia had this robotic creature shipped to us when the foolish children all boarded their flights to Israel," said Dr. Ivanovich. "Are you familiar with it?"

"Yes," said Ms. Kaplan. "They call him Leo. He is a very advanced, artificially intelligent automaton."

"Is it of any use to us? Or should I have it destroyed? Stripped for parts and components and then melted down?"

There was a pang of guilt in the pit of Tari Kaplan's stomach. What had she done? Leo or Lenard or whatever you wanted to call the mannequin-faced robot was an electronic marvel. Ms. Kaplan still loved science and technology. She still admired genius and ingenuity. She didn't want to see a creature this intricate, advanced, and exquisite destroyed.

She also wanted a shot at redemption for her evil acts.

"No," she said to Dr. Ivanovich. "We should not destroy

the robot. We should use him and his advanced AI to assist us."

"I don't know," said Dr. Ivanovich. "Perhaps you haven't been paying attention. We Fossils are not all that keen on new technology like this artificial intelligence you keep going on about. We prefer to make money from the old ways of doing things. Coal. Oil. Gas-powered cars. Destroy the robot." He started walking back up the arched stone corridor, his footfalls echoing with every step.

"I will make him a valuable asset, Dr. Ivanovich," Ms. Kaplan shouted after him. "I swear I will. You will not regret letting me work with the robot."

Dr. Ivanovich kept walking. He didn't turn around. But he did give Ms. Kaplan a dismissive backward wave of his hand.

"Fine. Whatever. Waste your time. Our bank accounts are fat and happy. Turn your little boy-bot into a 'valuable asset.' Maybe I can use him to count all my new money."

Now he stopped and turned around to glare at Ms. Kaplan.

"But if you end up wasting my time, Ms. Kaplan, you will pay. You will pay dearly."

"Of course, Dr. Ivanovich," she said with a slight and humble bow. "I understand completely."

The doctor walked away.

And Tari Kaplan hoped she remembered some of the things young Klaus had taught her about how to program and operate the automaton.

Leo could be her chance to make right at least some of the wrongs she had done.

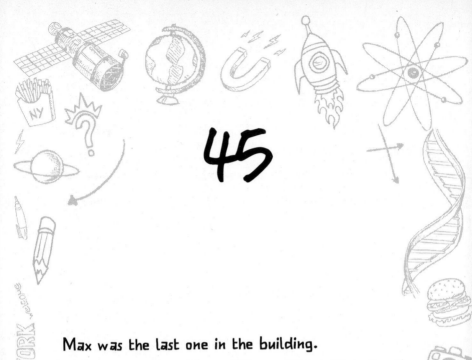

45

Max was the last one in the building.

Siobhan, Keeto, Toma, Vihaan, Klaus, Tisa, Annika, Anna, and Alexei had all shuttled off to Tel Aviv for the first of the flights that would, eventually, take them all home.

Home.

Where exactly is that going to be? Max wondered.

If only she could perfect her time-traveling abilities. Then she could head back to 1921 and her cozy home in Princeton, New Jersey. It was the only one she'd ever known. And she'd only known it for less than a year.

Here in the present, burly movers were wrapping furniture in moving blankets strapped in tight with screeching rolls of duct tape. Computer terminals were going into cardboard cartons filled with foam peanuts. There were no more photographs or art on the walls, just faded rectangles where they used to hang.

"Hello, Max."

Ben came out of what had been his office toting a cardboard box filled with file folders.

"Here," he said, balancing the box on his knee so he could search through the files. "This is for you."

He handed Max a brown envelope with a string-tied flap.

"What is it?" Max asked.

"A key to your old apartment over the horse stables. Well, you know, the renovated version. The one we fixed up for you."

"I thought your banks took everything."

"They did. Everything they could touch. Fortunately, the Stables apartment complex for low-income renters is owned by a charitable trust. Not me. Mr. Kennedy says your old place is vacant. So, uh, it's yours. For as long as you need or want it."

Max felt the "where am I going to live?" knot loosen in her gut. She had feared she'd be homeless. Sure, she'd done it before. But she wasn't eager to do it again.

"How about you, Ben?" she asked. "Where will you go?"

"Someplace else the bankers couldn't touch. My family has a compound on the coast in Maine. We've owned it free and clear for several generations and, thanks to some very high-priced lawyers I could never afford to hire again, it's another asset my so-called creditors can't touch."

"What happened, Ben? How could you lose everything so quickly?"

"I'm not one hundred percent certain, Max. Annika, Keeto, and Klaus think I might've been hacked by what they call 'bad actors.' They insist on doing some forensic accounting. They want to try to help me figure it out. If and when we do, Keeto says we're going to, and I quote, 'wreak cyber revenge on the fools who did you dirty.' How about you, Max? What'll you do next?"

Max shrugged. "I haven't really thought about it. I was still trying to work out the whole 'where am I going to sleep' thing. Now that that's taken care of, maybe I'll pick up where I left off. Drop in on some classes at NYU or Columbia..."

"Don't hide your light for too long."

"Huh?"

"You have so much to offer the world."

"Maybe," said Max. "But, right now, it doesn't seem like the world is all that interested in anything I might do or say. I'm just the dumb genius who sprayed salt water up into the air in Australia."

Ben and Max had one last snack together.

In the empty break room where they sat on cardboard boxes and ate whatever was left in the CMI fridge.

When their light meal was done and their stomachs felt queasy, Ben said, "I'll have my driver run you out to the airport."

"That's okay," said Max. "I'll just grab a cab. I have enough cash."

She didn't want to be the one to remind Ben that he didn't have a driver or a car anymore.

46

Max's flight home to New York City from Tel Aviv
wasn't nearly as glamorous as her first flight from New York
to Tel Aviv.

Back then she flew in Ben's private jet.

Now, she flew on a commercial airliner, crammed into
a middle seat in the back of the plane, way too close to the
toilets. She didn't even have her own armrests. (She had to
share them with her neighbors, both of whom were too fast
asleep to share anything.)

Max hadn't checked any bags for the flight. All of her
current possessions fit into a small duffel bag. A change or

two of clothes. A toothbrush. And one bobblehead Einstein doll she'd bought at a gift shop in the airport.

She also had her string-tied envelope from Ben. The keys and paperwork she'd need to move into her new (rent-free!) apartment in the Stables.

The flight on El Al would take about twelve hours. Half a day.

Plenty of time to think about everything that had gone wrong. How trying to do good in the world had led to so much bad.

"Did it, though?" asked the Einstein voice in her head. "Did it really? As I recall, you and your friends brought electricity to a village in Africa. You brought clean water to a small town in India. You even made a dent in the world hunger crisis by mapping out the logistics of food distribution in a small corner of West Virginia. An example, by the way, that many are now replicating..."

"I guess," Max mumbled sourly to herself. She was definitely feeling down in the dumps.

"So you've had a few setbacks," said her internal Einstein.

"Setbacks? Ben is broke. The CMI is over. My friends are all scattered to the wind."

"True. But, as I once wrote to Auguste Hochberger—"

"Who?"

"Someone I corresponded with when I lived in Berlin in 1919. Look it up."

"I will."

"Anyway, as I was saying, I once wrote to Herr Hochberger the following: 'Failure and deprivation are the best educators and purifiers.'"

"In other words," said Max, "we can all learn from our mistakes."

"Precisely."

"Then I guess I learned that it's pointless to try to do good in the world."

"Ach! Enough with the pity party. Do I need to repeat your recent accomplishments again, Ms. Einstein? Africa, India, West Virginia..."

"But those things were so small relative to the whole world's problems."

"Perhaps. But to the people you helped? Those same small things were enormous."

Max grinned. "Everything always comes back to your theory of relativity."

"*Ja.* It's a good one. And $E=mc^2$. 'Energy equals mass times the speed of light squared.' That's another good formula to remember. It shows us that a very small amount of mass may be converted into a very large, almost immeasurable amount of energy. These little things you do, Max? They can be converted into massive results."

Now Max was nodding.

She was also remembering that thing Alexei had said: *"Sometimes, the big solution is lots of little solutions."*

Maybe Max and her friends weren't done fighting global warming.

Maybe they didn't need a bunch of money to inject a million tons of sulfur dioxide into the stratosphere.

What if the CMI attacked the climate crisis the same way they tackled their other projects? Start small. Inspire others. Watch those little seeds explode like the speed of light squared.

"I think you've got this, Max," said the Einstein in her head.

"Yeah. I think I do."

The breaking up of the CMI and sending its team of young geniuses off to the far-flung corners of the globe might turn out to be the best thing that ever happened to the group.

What if the ten members reached out to ten people who

reached out to ten more people who reached out to ten more until there were thousands of small global warming solutions being demonstrated, all on the same day?

And then the lightning bolt of inspiration hit.

April twenty-second.

Earth Day.

That's when everybody would show the world how they were taking small steps to save that world.

Max was glad Klaus had given her a new phone.

She had some calls to make when she landed.

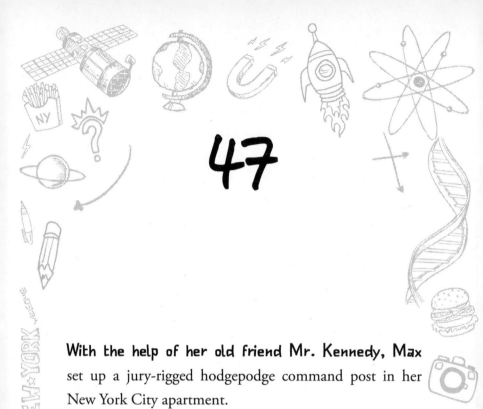

47

With the help of her old friend Mr. Kennedy, Max set up a jury-rigged hodgepodge command post in her New York City apartment.

"The router and cables came from various dumpsters around town," said Mr. Kennedy as he completed wiring everything together. "The computer? Well, I built that from spare parts I've been scavenging over the past few months. It's amazing what people toss to the curb when they buy something shiny and new."

Mr. Kennedy had been one of the homeless squatters living in the freezing-cold spaces above the horse stables when Max was a homeless squatter herself. Now Mr. Kennedy

had a job at the Apple Store Genius Bar. He also had one of the warm and cozy efficiency apartments in the renovated building called the Stables that Ben had financed, back when Ben had money to finance stuff.

"The Wi-Fi here is fantastic," Mr. Kennedy told Max. "We're running mesh routers on fiber optic cable throughout the building."

Max quickly composed and sent out a group text to all her former teammates:

"We're only done if we stop doing good in the world," she wrote to them.

She added a link to an interview with Christiana Figueres, the architect of the historic 2015 Paris Agreement on global warming.

The interview was reprinted in *The Ecologist*, a journal. In it, Figueres saw two possible choices for the future of life on Earth in the year 2050.

One would lead to a world on fire where coral reefs had vanished, sea levels had risen nearly eight inches, and millions of desperate people had been forced to migrate from areas so ravaged by global warming that no one could live in them any longer.

The second would be a world where emissions had been

halved every decade since 2020, cities had been transformed by mass tree-planting, and high-speed rail had replaced domestic flights while creating jobs.

"It's easy to give up and see a dark, dystopian future as the only possibility," Max wrote. "But it would be foolish to give up on the possibility, no matter how remote, of a happier ending. Right, Alexei?"

Max finished her message to her former teammates with a final quote from Christiana Figueres: "Stubborn optimism needs to motivate you daily; you always need to bear in mind why you feel the future is worth fighting for."

And then Max added her own closing thoughts.

"The future is worth fighting for because we're the ones who are going to live there. We will always own more of that particular stretch of time than our parents or grandparents. This decade is a moment of choice unlike any other. It may be our last chance to turn things around. The planet is running out of time. So are we. But I'm stubbornly optimistic about our chances. So let's all do what we can, no matter how small, to fight for the future we want and deserve. Let's all do it at once. On Earth Day, April 22, let's get others to join in with us. Let's take so many baby steps that, together, they become a giant leap! Let's do this thing!"

Everybody was on board with the plan.

They'd each find something "small" they could do.

They'd pressure their parents into finding ways to power their homes with renewable energy. They'd weatherize those homes, too, sealing drafts and adding insulation to cut down on heating and air-conditioning.

They'd look for energy-efficient appliances.

They'd waste less water.

They'd turn down the thermostat and rediscover sweaters, blankets, and cozy socks.

They'd buy better bulbs and actually eat more of the food they brought home from the grocery store.

They'd ride their bikes more.

They'd recycle.

They'd showcase it all on Earth Day. They'd recruit others to do the same.

Even Klaus was on board.

"Leo finally convinced me," he told Max in a private text thread. "He gave me a massive data dump revealing the truth. The science is staggering, especially when you filter out all the bogus stuff bought and paid for by the fossil fuel industries. Leo says we need to fight global warming because there is no Planet B. I think he's machine-learning how to be funny."

"That's great!" Max texted back. "Where did you find him?"

"I didn't," Klaus replied. "Leo found me. Someone must've unpacked and rebooted him. He's up and running and sending me messages when he can. I think he's someplace bad, Max. Someplace where he's under constant surveillance. So, here's the deal—once we save the planet, we still need to save Leo."

48

The CMI team went to work all around the globe.

They came up with simple things they could do.

And then they recruited others to do simple things and to recruit even more kids to the cause.

Max reached out to the Sunrise Movement, a group that proclaimed on their website "We Are the Climate Revolution." It was a youth crusade dedicated to stopping climate change while creating millions of good jobs in the process. They were an army of young people pushing to make the fight against global warming an urgent priority all across America. Most members were under the age of thirty. And they were totally down with Max's Earth Day plans. They even liked what the CMI had tried to do in Australia. "Just because it looks stupid on TV doesn't mean it's a dumb idea."

Once the ball was rolling, Max started focusing on her own small-step initiative. She was going to paint some rooftops white in New York City. Installing white roofs would make them reflect back more sunlight and reduce heat buildup in the city. She found some research that showed replacing dark surfaces with white ones could lower heat-wave maximum temperatures by two degrees Celsius or more. A white roof on top of the Stables would stop it from becoming part of an "urban heat island."

Out in California, Keeto would be working with some friends and family to coat their neighborhood's streets with a light-gray paint engineered to reduce blacktop temperatures.

"The earth was a lot cooler back when we had more grass than asphalt," Keeto told Max. "But we can't go back to that. Where would we all drive our electric cars?"

In India, Vihaan was working with an army of new-energy entrepreneurs.

"We're going to show off our electric rickshaws," he told Max excitedly. "There are almost two million of them here in India—more than the total number of electric cars sold in the US. It's a homegrown success story. I hope I speak for all of India when I say we are tired of being the planet's third-largest emitter of carbon dioxide. Rickshaws to the rescue!"

In China, Toma was trying to do something small but significant to, hopefully, help his nation stop being the world's biggest source of greenhouse gas emissions. "We're going to plant trees to help increase the forest coverage outside Beijing. Lots and lots of trees! Trees pump out oxygen to make up for all the smog being pumped out of Beijing."

Tisa and her friends would be installing even more solar panels in Africa.

And Siobhan was having fun back home in Ireland. She and her family were busy promoting April 22 as National Shorter Shower Day.

On April 21, Mr. Kennedy knocked on Max's door just as she was finishing up a conversation with Klaus. Klaus was also going to be planting trees in Poland on Earth Day. Except he wouldn't be doing the digging or planting. He'd built a team of robots to do the sweaty job for him. "Solar-powered robots."

"We better head over to the hardware store," said Mr. Kennedy when Max opened her door. "Tomorrow's the big day."

"A big day full of small steps," said Max. She grabbed

her light jacket and followed Mr. Kennedy down to the lobby so they could take the subway to the Home Depot store downtown. It wasn't hard to raise the money for the paint and painting supplies. Everybody in the building and around the neighborhood chipped in what they could and, soon, they had enough. Just another example of a big solution coming from a lot of little ones.

"So, you're going to video us doing our thing up on the roof?" Mr. Kennedy asked on the ride downtown.

"Yep," said Max. "And then we're going to post that video clip all over the internet and social media. Everybody else is going to do the same. The CMI kids. The Sunrise Movement. Everybody. The marketing maven who was working with us in Australia, Anna Sophia Fiorillo, will be in charge of making sure we get the maximum play in the major media, too. This Earth Day fight to reverse global warming is going, well, *global*!"

Mr. Kennedy arched an eyebrow and stroked his chin. "People everywhere are going to watch what we're doing up on that roof?"

"Yes, sir. Well, we sure hope they are."

Mr. Kennedy nodded. "Then I guess I better shave tomorrow morning."

49

Dr. Ivanovich tramped down the damp stone corridor of his mountaintop headquarters.

He was squeezing the pair of diamonds in his fist so tightly veins were bulging out around his knuckles. Ms. Kaplan and Leo the robot were toddling along behind him, doing their best to keep up with his hurried pace.

"Why didn't your 'very sophisticated' robot pick up all this chatter?" Dr. Ivanovich demanded of Ms. Kaplan. "His so-called artificial intelligence is a joke. He should've known about this! Now it might be too late."

"I'm so sorry, sir," said Ms. Kaplan, sounding for all the world like a groveling toady. "If I had known you were

interested in Leo's advanced communications surveillance capabilities…"

"Never mind!" Seething, Dr. Ivanovich lurched into a dim chamber illuminated by the faint glow of computer monitors and the blinking LEDs from racks of servers and routers. He flapped his arms at all the screens. "We'll deal with this the way we know best."

"What is all of this?" Ms. Kaplan asked, innocently, because she had absolutely no idea why Dr. Ivanovich was so furious.

"More meddling in our affairs. Brought on, it seems, by your friend Max Einstein."

"She isn't my friend."

"Very well. Your former pupil. She and all the other sniveling whiners from that Change Makers Institute have scattered across the globe and are currently planning small global warming demonstrations on a massive scale for tomorrow, April twenty-second."

"Earth Day," mumbled Ms. Kaplan.

"Yes. Very clever. I'm sure that bratty young marketing wizard they added to their team came up with that cute idea. 'Protect the Earth on Earth Day.' So trite. So predictable."

"I'm sure Leo knew nothing about this," said Ms. Kaplan.

Leo remained silent.

"Well, he should've known something! You've had him hooked up to an ethernet cable for days."

Leo finally piped up. "I was downloading several software updates, Dr. Ivanovich. As you probably know, that is a tedious and time-consuming operation, especially as I am programmed to read and analyze all the fine print in the license agreements and—"

"Silence!" Irate, Dr. Ivanovich actually threw his two bird-egg-sized stones to the floor where the diamonds etched a pair of angry gashes. "I have work to do."

He clasped his hand on the shoulder of a technician clacking at a keyboard. The technician froze. It was as if Dr. Ivanovich's hand were made of ice. Instagram posts and tweets and boxes filled with text doom-scrolled down the young man's screen. Dr. Ivanovich squeezed the man's shoulder blade hard.

"Nikolai?"

"*Da?*"

"Kindly give me an update on our situation."

"Things have gotten worse, sir. Thousands of young people all over the world are joining in the plans. They are calling what they are doing small but mighty steps toward the end of global warming. None of these steps are very kind to the fossil fuel industry. Neither are the protest slogans. These are just some of the posts. They're scrolling that rapidly in real time. Several climate change activist groups have also taken up the cause sparked by Ms. Einstein's initial postings. They are calling this Operation Stubborn Optimism. There will be events and rallies and demonstrations throughout the day."

"Have you contacted the Web brigades?"

Nikolai nodded. "*Da*. The entire Russian troll army with all its bot farms is at our disposal. They will flood the Web and manipulate online views and opinions. We will quickly turn the world against these young socialist do-gooders aiming to sabotage the global economy."

"Excellent. I thought we were done with these foolish children. Apparently I was wrong."

"We will be soon, sir," said Nikolai.

Now Dr. Ivanovich's assistant, Vlad, came into the room.

"There is an assassin available in London," he reported. "Unfortunately, he has a prior commitment for tomorrow and will be unable to travel to New York City and eliminate Max Einstein until the twenty-third at the earliest."

"Do we have any assets currently in New York?"

"Yes," said Vlad. "No trained killers, but several very skilled operatives. Excellent infiltrators and imposters. They could do some dirty tricks for us. Maybe get Max Einstein on TV again."

Vlad and Ivanovich shared a knowing grin.

"Make it so," commanded the doctor. "If we can embarrass Ms. Einstein on a global scale as we did down in Australia it might be a better play than killing her. She is the head of this movement. Its face. So let's turn her into a laughingstock and watch the movement crumble beneath her as she has another very public epic fail."

"I'm on it," said Vlad, leaving the room and jabbing a phone number into his satellite phone.

"What about us?" asked Ms. Kaplan timidly. She gestured half-heartedly to Leo. "I'm curious as to why you summoned us. Is there anything we can do to help you in this situation?"

"Yes, Ms. Kaplan. First, you can tell me everything you know about Maxine Einstein. Especially anything dealing with her past. Then, you can destroy your ridiculous, utterly useless robot. He looks like a runaway mannequin from a department store. I don't like his smile. I detest his shiny swoop of black hair. And I can't stand his ineptitude. Harvest any parts that might prove useful in the future and then rip out his wires and melt down his plastic shell. I never want to see that smirking face again!"

50

"**Is it true you're up here on this roof because you're** trying to overthrow the fossil fuel patriarchy?" shouted a reporter.

"What?" said Max, shocked by the question.

She and her whole roof-painting crew were totally out-numbered by the gaggle of reporters and cameras that had joined them up on the roof of the Stables apartment build-ing. Anna had orchestrated all sorts of media attention for the Earth Day demonstrations. But this wasn't the kind of attention Max had been hoping for.

"When did you become a communist, Ms. Einstein?" shouted another.

"A communist? Who said—"

"It's all over Facebook and Twitter. Instagram and Snapchat, too."

"Are you the head of this international cabal of kids stirring up trouble all over the world?" cried a woman jabbing a microphone toward Max.

"Are you people crazy?" snapped Mr. Kennedy, holding a dripping paint roller on a pole as if it were a valiant knight's lance. "A cabal is a secret political clique or faction trying to promote their private views. You fools know what Max and her friends are doing, so, therefore, it isn't secret. And they've been very public about their views. How can she be part of a cabal? Come on. You're journalists. Use your words. Okay, Max. Tell 'em what we're doing up here."

Max nodded. She almost inadvertently gestured with her roller to use it as a pointer but then she thought better of it. She didn't want to splatter the press with paint, no matter how infuriating and misinformed their questions were.

By the way, who was spreading all these lies about her on social media?

Was somebody doing a TikTok making fun of her, too?

Stationed behind the wall of reporters, the formerly homeless Mrs. Rabinowitz gave Max a big thumbs-up.

She was standing on a five-gallon orange bucket using Max's phone to livestream the rooftop painting party to the World Wide Web. Mrs. Rabinowitz had a huge smile on her face. She was quite delighted with herself. She'd never streamed anything live to the World Wide Web but Max had shown her what buttons to push. Once Mrs. Rabinowitz knew what to do, she said it was easy-peasy.

Max was very aware that millions of people might be listening to what she said next. Her big Earth Day "small steps" activism initiative was in full swing and she was about to play a starring role in it.

"We're just doing our small part, here on Earth Day, to help reduce global warming," she told the assembled media. "By painting a few rooftops in our New York City neighborhood white, we can reduce the solar radiation these buildings absorb, which means less heat will be transferred downstairs. And that means we'll need less electricity to run air conditioners."

Max kept going. "This clean white roof will reflect eighty percent of sunlight and—"

"Aren't you taking jobs away from air-conditioner repair people?" demanded a reporter from New York's most notorious tabloid newspaper.

"Actually," said Max, "we're creating jobs."

"How? You're not getting paid to do this, are you?"

"No," said Max. "Of course not. We're volunteers. All the kids around the world taking small but mighty steps to combat global warming today are volunteers."

"So, if you kids are all doing the work for free, how does that create jobs?"

"It will. In the future."

"Well, a lot of those air-conditioner repair people need money, now!"

And that's when a man carrying a clipboard pushed his way through the mob of reporters.

He was followed by an officer from the NYPD.

Neither one of them looked very pleased with Max's paint job.

51

"I'm an inspector with the New York City Department of Buildings and Roofs," said the man with the clipboard.

He had that bored, no-nonsense, let's-get-this-over-with attitude of a municipal worker who hated his job.

"This gentleman to my right is with the NYPD."

The police officer crossed his arms in front of his belt buckle and stood up a little straighter. He had a barrel chest and beefy, tattooed arms. He also had a service weapon in his holster.

"You're Maxine Einstein, is that correct?" said the inspector.

"Yes."

"The same Max Einstein who sprayed salt water up into the clouds in Australia." The inspector actually smiled a little when he said that.

The reporters and TV camera crews jostled forward a little the instant the inspector mentioned the Australian fiasco.

"Oh, yeah," Max heard a couple of them say. "Forgot about that little stunt. That was hilarious..."

"Yes, sir," Max told the reporter. "But this really has nothing to do with the CMI effort at cloud brightening over the Great Barrier Reef."

"Uh-huh," said the inspector, ticking some box on his clipboard sheet. "Tell me, Ms. Einstein, have you taken the city's CoolRoofs training program?"

"No. I didn't know there was a—"

"Are you authorized and certified to install the officially sanctioned energy-saving reflective surface as part of the CoolRoofs initiative?"

"This is just paint," said Max.

"And is this surface granulated cap sheet, asphalt, or modified bitumen?"

"I think it's, you know, tar..."

"Is there a three-foot, eight-inch parapet?"

"We actually didn't measure the, uh, parapet. We just started painting."

The inspector shook his head and let out a long, disappointed sigh. "Ms. Einstein, I'd heard you were smart. Well, smart kids usually do their homework. There are rules and requirements that must be adhered to." He ripped the sheet of paper out of his clipboard.

"This is a cease-and-desist order. You are hereby directed to stop painting this roof, pack up your equipment, leave, and never come back. Unless, of course, you complete the appropriate training program. I understand it's a free class. Something you're used to. You used to drop in on college classes at NYU without paying tuition, am I right?"

Max narrowed her eyes.

How could a building inspector for New York City possibly know that random piece of trivia from my past?

The burly cop stepped forward. "You heard the inspector, little lady. Pack up and move out."

Feeling defeated, Max and her crew of friends and neighbors started gathering up their paint gear. The TV cameras pushed in for close-ups of Max as she toted a heavy tub of paint. Cameras flashed. The reporters swapped jokes, chuckled, and shook their heads.

"She really does some dumb stuff for such a smart kid," Max heard one of them say.

"Geniuses," said another. "They ain't got no common sense."

Max hauled her bucket over to the bulkhead door that opened into the stairwell. The inspector and police officer were both right there. Smiling.

"You ready to move back to Little Angels, your old orphanage out in Brooklyn?" asked the cop. "I'm sure they could find a bed for you."

"I have an apartment in this building," Max replied. "It's in my name."

"Is that so," said the building inspector, licking the tip of his pencil, as if he were getting ready to jot down a note. "What are you? Twelve? Thirteen?"

Max didn't answer. She had a pretty good idea where the man was going.

"You know you have to be at least eighteen to sign a lease in New York City."

"I know," said Max. "That's why I bought it outright instead of renting. Excuse me."

She pushed her way past the two men and carried the paint bucket downstairs to her apartment where she locked and bolted the door.

She went to the front window and looked out.

The media were still down there, in a tight clump around the building's front door.

They were eager to capture more footage of the humiliated Max Einstein.

Max slumped down on the edge of the bed.

She looked at her phone. The social media feeds were filled with lies and falsehoods and pictures of the building inspector shutting down Max Einstein's "unlawful rooftop paint party."

The phone buzzed. Max nearly jumped out of her skin.

It was a text.

From Klaus in Poland.

"Heads-up," it read. "Leo tells me you're about to meet a fake building inspector and a phony cop."

Max quickly tapped in a reply: "I knew there was something fishy about those two! What's going on?"

"Leo's been gathering a ton of intelligence behind enemy lines. A group of oil oligarchs based in the Ural Mountains is trying to destroy you and everything you, me, and just about every other kid in the world is trying to do. They've been trolling you, Max. Sending out all sorts of disinformation with the help of Russian bot farms. Leo's been monitoring the situation. He has the receipts for their dirty deeds. Ms. Kaplan is helping them. Sort of. She's dishing dirt on you and your past. Leo recorded everything. We can take these goons down like we took down the Corp."

"Is Leo safe?"

"Almost."

"Where is he?"

"Precisely where he needs to be."

52

For maybe the first time ever, Klaus inspired Max.

Actually, that wasn't true. Klaus was pretty amazing and inspiring whenever he was working on robots. But it was what he'd just said about Leo that made Max realize she had better things to do than sit on the edge of her bed moping.

"Precisely where he needs to be."

Max needed to do the same thing. The time for hiding was over. She needed to be downstairs, facing the music, keeping the media focused on all the awesome Earth Day projects and demonstrations taking place all over the globe.

She reached for her phone to check on the latest status reports.

266

Alerts started binging and bonging like crazy.

All the social media attacks making fun of the young people spending their day fighting global warming were now flagged with warnings:

"This post originated in a Russian troll farm."

"This is explicit misinformation."

"This tweet violates Twitter rules."

"Click this link to get the facts on global Earth Day demonstrations."

Was Leo behind this sudden change?

Had Klaus's super-bot somehow outsmarted all the Russian bots toiling away in their troll farms?

Was the automaton even better at shifting public opinion than Anna Sophia Fiorillo?

Now there were all sorts of positive posts.

"Keep up the good work, kids!"

"Time to take back our future!"

"Don't burn fossils or you'll end up one!"

"We need your resistance to save our existence!"

Energized, Max dashed downstairs to address the mob of media still milling around in front of the Stables. And on the way, she pulled out her phone and did some quick research on CoolRoofs.

"Hi, guys," she said to the reporters. "You know what? I am going to take that CoolRoofs class. I think that's a great thing that New York City has done. Sure, it's pretty simple, but multiplied by the power of a million New Yorkers, it becomes huge. Remember what Einstein said. E=mc²."

There was a collective "Huh?" expression on the reporters' faces so Max explained.

"Even something as small as an atom can unleash unlimited energy."

Now the reporters were staring at her. None were asking nasty questions.

"So, yeah. I'm going to get officially certified and then go back upstairs and finish what we started today. Because it's time we all started making changes to fight climate change. You know what else my hero Professor Albert Einstein said ninety years ago? 'The destiny of civilized humanity depends more than ever on the moral forces it is capable of generating.' I guess every century humanity gets faced with a destiny-shaping choice. For him, it was the atom bomb. For us, it's global warming. So, starting today, we all need to generate all sorts of moral force and rise to the challenge."

What happened next shocked Max.

Apparently, some of the TV cameras were livestreaming her remarks on the internet. Either that, or Leo was hard at work spreading Max's short but surprisingly inspirational speech.

Because, when she went back inside to fill out her Cool-Roofs application, her computer's news feed was full of footage of kids taking to the streets with homemade protest signs. They were accompanied by their teachers and parents, too. Millions of individual voices were coming together in a resounding chorus. And it wasn't just happening in America. There were protests in Brazil, Japan, Korea, Kenya, even Russia.

Then came another surprise: a team of certified NYC CoolRoofs contractors showed up at the Stables, went up to the top of Max's building, and finished what she, Mr. Kennedy, and the others had started.

"We heard what you said, Miss Einstein," the lead contractor told her. "When you quoted your grandpa Albert Einstein."

"He's not my grandpa."

"Okay. Your great-grandfather. Whatever. The guy was right. We dropped by to generate a little moral force here. In fact, when we get done with your building, we're moving next door and doing that one, too. For free. How's that for some of that moral force action you were talking about?"

Max spent the rest of Earth Day up on the roofs of the neighborhood with the contractor and his crew. In between paint jobs, she checked her phone.

She was thrilled to see so many young people coming together, shouting slogans and carrying signs.

You are destroying our future! was written in red on many of the banners and placards.

Others proclaimed Our house is on fire! The Climate Is Changing, Why Aren't We? and Climate Change Is Worse Than Homework.

But the one Max liked the best only needed three words: It's Our Future.

The future was definitely something worth fighting for.

Even if Max Einstein herself secretly longed to skip the future so she could return to the past.

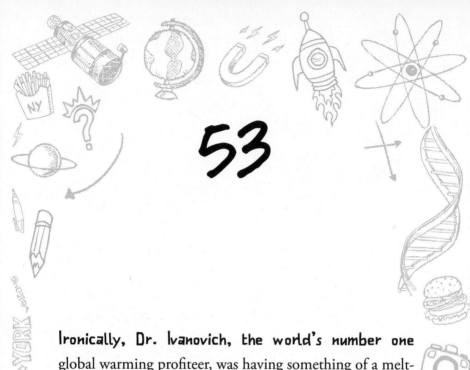

53

Ironically, Dr. Ivanovich, the world's number one global warming profiteer, was having something of a meltdown as he watched the climate change actions and protests sweeping around the globe.

He was furiously clicking and clacking his twin diamonds in his clenched fist, watching nothing but positive posts streaming across the screens in his command bunker.

"Nikolai?" he wondered out loud. "Why are the Russian Web brigades and the trolls at the Internet Research Agency sending out such glowing comments about these foolish children and their ridiculous antics?"

"I am not one hundred percent certain, Dr. Ivanovich."

"Then guess, Nikolai! Guess!"

Nikolai swallowed hard. "It appears, in my estimation, that our bots have been overridden by, perhaps, an even more powerful army of highly sophisticated robotic disruptors."

"Or just one," said a voice behind them.

Leo, the annoying robot with the childish face, stepped into the command-and-control center.

He wasn't alone.

A small squad of military commandos, all of them dressed in black and carrying a multitude of lethal weapons, bustled into the room behind the grinning automaton.

"These are my friends, Charl and Isabl," Leo said calmly. "I sent them a distress signal. They've come to rescue me. These other individuals, I believe, are their friends."

Charl and Isabl stepped forward. Their assault weapons were casually draped across their chests. The seven steely-eyed commandos behind them had their weapons up. Most of them were trained on Dr. Ivanovich. One was pointed at Nikolai.

"We have already secured your assistant, Vlad, in one of our helicopters," said the woman named Isabl.

"These other ladies and gentlemen," said Charl, "are

members of Mossad. Our former colleagues at the Israeli intelligence agency."

"We used to work with them," added Isabl. "Until Ben hired us to keep an eye on the Change Maker kids. But then, well, somebody tinkered with Ben's bank accounts..."

"That was Dr. Ivanovich," said Leo. "I can show you the data..."

Isabl shrugged. "Maybe later, Leo. Anyway, when we got pinged by Leo's distress signal—which, by the way, uses GPS coordinates to pinpoint his precise location—we called up our old friends and colleagues at Mossad and, together, we decided to come after you."

"You have to try to keep busy when you're retired," said Charl.

Dr. Ivanovich was fuming. "How dare you people barge into my home like this!"

"This is your home?" said Isabl. Then she whistled. "I'm impressed. How many rooms are in this castle? A hundred? Two hundred?"

"I insist that you people lower your weapons and leave or I will be forced to summon the local authorities."

Charl shook his head. "Nah. That's not going to work.

We already talked to them. They say you're like the planet. You're way too hot."

"Especially since Pavel Zakhar Victorovich, the assassin you hired to eliminate Max Einstein, talked," said a member of the Mossad squad. "In fact, the Skull told us everything."

"Ha!" Dr. Ivanovich laughed. "You have absolutely no way to connect this so-called assassin with me."

"Actually," said Leo, "while hooked up to your very speedy ethernet network, I was able to access all your encrypted communication files and put together a chain of evidence directly linking you to the hiring of this gentleman known as 'the Skull.' An odd and unflattering nickname for sure, but he has confessed to the attempted crime and now, thanks to my data mining, there is more than enough documented evidence to indict you on several counts of attempted murder for hire in the sovereign state of Israel."

"That's what the judge in Tel Aviv said when he issued this warrant for your arrest and extradition," said Charl. "And your friends at the Kremlin? They're not so friendly anymore, Doc. Oh, by the way. They want your diamonds.

They plan to put them on display in their Fabergé Museum next to all those Imperial Eggs."

Dr. Ivanovich spun around in his swivel chair to glare at Leo.

"Where is Ms. Kaplan? She and I need to talk."

"She already talked," said Isabl. "To us. That's why she's heading home to Israel. Says she wants to atone for her sins, which she'll probably be doing in a prison cell for the next year or two."

Dr. Ivanovich was seething. "You did this to me!" he snapped at Leo. "I should've tossed you into the trash heap the minute you arrived on my loading dock. I should've crushed you in a trash compactor!"

"Yes," said Leo, with a smug smile. "You probably should have. But, unfortunately for you, you did not. For, you see, Dr. Ivanovich, I was initially designed by the Corp to be rather nefarious and villainous. In fact, my original purpose was to work with Max Einstein on a revolutionary new kind of quantum computer. The Corp programmed me to learn everything I could from Max. In short, they initially created me to be an espionage bot. A spy."

"And so you spied on me."

"Exactly, sir! My friend Klaus, working remotely from

his home in Poland, was able to tap into and reboot my incredible spy craft capabilities and software. It's just something that's hardwired into my coding, Dr. Ivanovich. It's nothing personal. But, unfortunately, you're toast."

And then Leo giggled. Just like he used to when the Corp called him Lenard.

54

As Earth Day ended in New York City, Max was feeling great.

She was also a little achy.

She and her friends—new and old—had rolled out white reflective paint on half a dozen rooftops in the neighborhood. And no bogus building inspectors or phony cops showed up to give them any grief. All across the planet young people had stepped up. They'd shown the whole world their Stubborn Optimism. They refused to give up hope that tomorrow could be a better day.

If only every day could be like this Earth Day, thought

Max, *with people all over making small baby steps that, together, could lead to a giant reversal of global warming.*

It was a start.

And, today, that was good enough.

The Change Makers Institute might be closed down but kids all over the world had become the *new* change makers. With any luck, they'd keep doing whatever they could to teach the older generations how to do what, deep down, everybody knew was right. The people who had injured the planet should help save it.

And, like Albert Einstein said, "The destiny of civilized humanity depends more than ever on the moral forces it is capable of generating."

"Well, sir," Max said out loud, "today we generated all sorts of moral forces. You were right. It's amazing how much energy even the smallest particle or person can generate."

She raised her glass of bubbly brown soda.

"Here's to the speed of light squared!"

And that's when Albert Einstein appeared in Max's room.

The *real* Albert Einstein.

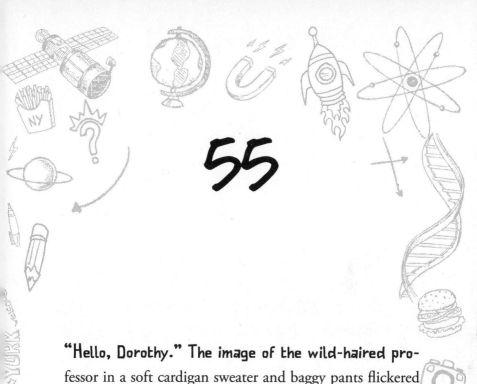

55

"Hello, Dorothy." The image of the wild-haired professor in a soft cardigan sweater and baggy pants flickered like a streaming video that didn't have quite enough Wi-Fi signal.

This wasn't the Einstein in her head. The one Max had imagined as her grandfatherly companion for so many years. She seldom "saw" that Einstein anywhere, except in the pictures she used to keep in her battered suitcase.

And that imaginary Einstein always called her Max, not Dorothy. Dorothy was the name of the toddler who'd gone missing in Princeton, New Jersey, way back in 1921 when, according to several sources, her parents were

tinkering with a time-travel device based on Einstein's theory of relativity.

Albert Einstein's image seemed to settle. He smoothed out his sweater. He patted his stomach.

"Yes. I am all here. This is remarkable..."

Max was too stunned to speak. But she tried. "Are you...you?"

"Oh, yes. Just as you are you. Of course, our notions of physical reality can never be final. I suppose all of physics is an attempt conceptually to grasp reality as something that is considered to be independent of its being observed. In this sense one speaks of 'physical reality.'"

Oh, yeah, thought Max, hearing that complex, mind-bending reply. *He's him. He's Albert Einstein.*

"How did...how..."

"Ah. How. My favorite question."

Einstein pulled up a chair, sat down, and crossed his legs.

He didn't glide through the seat. He wasn't a ghost. He was real.

"I will attempt to explain, Dorothy. Thanks to your extremely clever parents, Susan and Timothy, I have time-traveled from 1934 to what you perceive to be the present."

"1934?" said Max. "But, if what I've heard is true, I disappeared from Princeton in 1921. That's a thirteen-year difference…"

"*Ja.* Good use of your math. I knew you would be bright, Dorothy. A genius, perhaps? Well, how could you not be with parents as brilliant as Susan and Timothy? You see, my dear young friend, it took your parents those thirteen years after that first experiment to learn from their mistakes, adjust their methodology, build new equipment, and try again. There was, also, as you might suspect, a long period of grief in those intervening years. They missed you so much, Dorothy. They forsook science for five full years because they could not forgive themselves for what they had done back in 1921."

"They missed me?"

"Like the sun would miss the morning sky. So I encouraged them to try again. Not in Princeton. No. There were too many memories in that house. Bad memories. Awful memories. With the help of several very generous financial backers that I helped organize, Susan and Timothy built a new lab on the west side of Manhattan in some abandoned horse stables."

"What? They built their lab here? Right where I'd end up squatting and then living? That's impossible."

Einstein shrugged. "Impossible? What is impossible? Let us, instead, call it *schicksal*."

Max raised her confused eyebrows.

"I'm sorry," said Einstein. "That is German. It means destiny or fate. And even though I am an old fogey, I still refuse to believe that God plays dice with the universe. There must be a certain order to this world."

Max had a queasy feeling in the pit of her stomach.

She was almost too afraid to ask her next question.

But she took a deep breath and asked it.

"Sir, as much as I am beyond honored to be actually talking to you—I mean, you're my hero..."

Einstein blushed and bowed slightly. "*Danke.* Thank you."

"But why didn't my mother and father time-travel from 1934 to meet me? Why did you send you?"

Einstein smiled. There was a sly twinkle in his eye. The same twinkle Max had always imagined being there.

"Because, Dorothy, I insisted on going first. I was to be the, what do you call it? The guinea pig. After all, your parents' work is based on my theories. If those theoretical mind experiments proved to be a faulty foundation for their ingenious efforts, well, then I should be the one stranded forever on the time-space continuum. But do not worry. They will come into this future just as soon as I assure them that it is, indeed, possible."

Einstein began to flicker again.

"Ach! This straddling of space and time is limited to such short intervals. A leap forward, a temporary intersection, and then a return to the past where our existence is more firmly entrenched."

Another sputter was followed by a creak in the chair as Einstein's whole body shifted.

"Your parents will be here," he said, standing up. "Later today. Well before midnight."

"Seriously?" said Max, excitedly.

"Oh, yes. Today is April twenty-second, is it not?"

Max nodded.

"*Wunderbar*. You probably never knew this, Dorothy, but today, April twenty-second, is your birthday."

Knowing that nearly took Max's breath away. She had a birthday? Of course she did, but she'd never known when it was. She'd never had a birthday party.

Einstein began to fade.

"I'd love to stay and chat longer, Dorothy, but my time is up. Your mother and father will be arriving shortly. And guess what, Dorothy?"

"What?"

"They'll be bringing you your birthday cake."

ABOUT THE AUTHORS

For his prodigious imagination and championship of literacy in America, **James Patterson** was awarded the 2019 National Humanities Medal, and he has also received the Literarian Award for Outstanding Service to the American Literary Community from the National Book Foundation. He holds the Guinness World Record for the most #1 *New York Times* bestsellers, including *Max Einstein, Middle School, I Funny,* and *Jacky Ha-Ha,* and his books have sold more than 400 million copies worldwide. A tireless champion of the power of books and reading, Patterson created a children's book imprint, JIMMY Patterson, whose mission is simple: "We want every kid who finishes a JIMMY Book to say, 'PLEASE GIVE ME ANOTHER BOOK.'" He has donated more than three million books to students and soldiers and funds over four hundred Teacher and Writer Education Scholarships at twenty-one colleges and universities. He also supports 40,000 school libraries and has donated millions of dollars to independent bookstores. Patterson invests proceeds from the sales of JIMMY Patterson Books in pro-reading initiatives.

Chris Grabenstein is a *New York Times* bestselling author who has collaborated with James Patterson on the Max Einstein, I Funny, Jacky Ha-Ha, Treasure Hunters, and House of Robots series, as well as *Word of Mouse, Katt vs. Dogg, Pottymouth and Stoopid, Laugh Out Loud,* and *Daniel X: Armageddon.* He lives in New York City.

Jay Fabares is a freelance artist who specializes in character design, illustrations, and sequential art. Their most notable works have been as a development artist for Disney's Goldie & Bear and Puppy Dog Pals, as well as cover artist for Valiant Entertainment. Jay's passion project is her long-form webcomic that she co-writes with her husband, Sanders. Jay lives in sunny San Diego.